THE TIJUANA BIBLE READER

Borgo Press Books by VICTOR J. BANIS

*The Astral: Till the Day I Die * Avalon: An Historical Novel * The C.A.M.P. Cookbook * The C.A.M.P. Guide to Astrology * Charms, Spells, and Curses for the Millions * Color Him Gay: That Man from C.A.M.P. * The Curse of Bloodstone: A Gothic Novel of Terror * Darkwater: A Gothic Novel of Horror * The Daughters of Nightsong: An Historical Novel* (Nightsong Saga #2) * *The Devil's Dance: A Novel of Terror * Drag Thing; or, The Strange Tale of Jackle and Hyde * The Earth and All It Holds: An Historical Novel * A Family Affair: A Novel of Horror * Fatal Flowers: A Novel of Horror * Fire on the Moon: A Novel of Terror * The Gay Dogs: That Man from C.A.M.P. * The Gay Haunt * The Glass House: A Novel of Terror * The Glass Painting: A Gothic Tale of Horror * Goodbye, My Lover * The Greek Boy * The Green Rolling Hills: Writings from West Virginia* (editor) * *Green Willows: A Novel of Horror * Kenny's Back * Life & Other Passing Moments: A Collection of Short Writings * The Lion's Gate: A Novel of Terror * Love's Pawn: A Novel of Romance * Lucifer's Daughter: A Novel of Horror * Moon Garden: A Novel of Terror * Nightsong: An Historical Novel* (Nightsong Saga #1) * *The Pot Thickens: Recipes from Writers and Editors* (editor) * *San Antone: An Historical Novel * The Scent of Heather: A Novel of Terror * The Second House: A Novel of Terror * The Second Tijuana Bible Reader* (editor) * *The Sins of Nightsong: An Historical Novel* (Nightsong Saga #3) * *Spine Intact, Some Creases: Remembrances of a Paperback Writer * Stranger at the Door: A Novel of Suspense * Sweet Tormented Love: A Novel of Romance * The Sword and the Rose: An Historical Novel * This Splendid Earth: An Historical Novel * The Tijuana Bible Reader* (editor) * *Twisted Flames * The WATERCRESS File: That Man from C.A.M.P. * A Westward Love: An Historical Romance * White Jade: A Novel of Terror * The Why Not * The Wine of the Heart: A Novel of Romance * The Wolves of Craywood: A Novel of Terror*

THE TIJUANA BIBLE READER

AN ANTHOLOGY OF CLASSIC GAY STORIES

VICTOR J. BANIS,

EDITOR

THE BORGO PRESS

MMXII

THE TIJUANA BIBLE READER

DEDICATION

I am deeply indebted to my friend, Heather, for all the help she has given me in getting these early works of mine reissued.

And I am grateful as well to Rob Reginald, for all his assistance and support.

CONTENTS

FOREWORD

Tijuana Bibles...cock stories...crotch readers.... By what-ever appellation, these little gems are familiar to us all. What schoolboy has not traded them zealously with his classmates? What young man has not had them offered for sale as he made his way through the carnival, the amusement park, the county fair? They are a staple of the erotic arts, and particularly in this country, for, despite the south-of-the-border tag sometimes ap-plied to them, they are truly Americana. They are an aspect and a result of our rigid Puritan tradition that outlaws our inherent sexuality and forces us to derive the greater portion of our plea-sures from fantasies in lieu of reality. They reveal the American traditions of frustrated sexuality.

How did they come to be called Tijuana Bibles? In part because, while they are written for and by Americans, they are frequently printed and "bound" south of the border. Second, because the very use of the name Tijuana designates erotica and sexuality ; the erotic arts are specific.

Perhaps the most important reason lies in Tijuana's loca-tion, little more than spitting distance from San Diego. And San Diego is filled with men. Beautiful *young* men. Beautiful young servicemen. Beautiful, young, *horny* servicemen. In short, San Diego represents probably the world's largest market for mate-rial of this sort. And Tijuana, conveniently close across the border, provides a good place to have the material printed, etc.

Now, a great many such stories are prepared in places like Kalamazoo and Omaha. And every border town can produce a heady supply. But El Paso just doesn't have the numbers going for it that San Diego does. Nobody outside of the Pentagon can state exactly how many servicemen there are in San Diego, but it's well up in the multi-thousands. These guys are young and horny. They're a long way from their homes where, as often as not, stories such as these were a rarity and hard to come by (no pun intended). Most if not all of these guys end up sooner or later with a few of these readers in their possession.

Something else San Diego has got—queens. The gay boys flock there by the thousands also, for reasons which should be apparent from the above paragraph. And they too like erotica. Also, they like to share their erotica (etc.) with some of the handsome, horny young servicemen. There's lots of action in this town. It's known as "heaven" for chicken queens, those lascivious hawks who swoop down upon young prey. As a result, the erotica of San Diego runs lavender to a degree unknown anywhere else. In New York—not exactly a straight city—the percentage of gay versus straight material would be maybe ten out of a hundred. Elsewhere, it would be even less. But in San Diego, it's an easy fifty-fifty, maybe better. And if anybody still doubts a sexual revolution, let him contemplate on the fact that those figures are going up. Gay is in. And this is being reflected in erotica just as it is in major studio movies, best sellers, and cocktail party chatter.

The Tijuana Bibles offer a fascinating glimpse into the American male's sexual makeup. They mirror not only the changing times, as in the increase of homosexual acceptance, but virtually every form of sexual activity, and every attitude toward such behavior. Whatever aspect of sexuality one wishes to explore, it can be found here, as authentically presented and revealed as in any psychiatric case history. The fantasies through which man expresses his sexual longings are as telling as the "factual" accounts that he gives in the laboratory—perhaps more so. Here he utilizes the shield of anonymity, the freedom of literary exercise, the full strength of his imagination and the aid of erotic stimulation to demonstrate what he really feels, thinks, desires. Here are no cloaked meanings, no innuendoes, no carefully couched phrases designed to protect the ego. This is how it is, all the way inside, all guts and damn the general.

Every man ought to be able to enjoy these stories. They were written for that purpose, and what they have to say is not much different from what any of us would say if we let go the ropes.

Or, if you don't want to read them to enjoy them, you can study them, with a serious and scholarly intent. You'll get one hell of an education. Of course, you'd have gotten that anyway. But it seems a shame not to have both. And if you can't—or won't—enjoy them right along while you're studying them... well, maybe you ought to pause and ask yourself "why?"

That's the last bonus, you see. You just might find that even if you didn't like them, these little literary treasures provided a bit of therapy. They usually do. Sometimes it's that a guy lets off his steam reading them, and doesn't have the urge to go out afterward and molest anyone. And sometimes it's that he finally gets rid of a hang-up or two. And sometimes...well, like the guy who couldn't enjoy them a couple of paragraphs back; they kind of make him take a look at himself for a change.

And even that ain't bad.

—Victor J. Banis

CHAPTER ONE
ACT I, ACT II, ACT III

The structure of the erotic short story is always constant. The emphasis is placed upon action, and long descriptive passages or lengthy dialogue never finds a comfortable place in the basic outline of the story. The writing varies tremendously, from a few degrees above illiteracy to the greatest of writing talents.

In this, the first of the stories to be presented in this volume, the basic premise of the story is one which repeatedly creeps back into the erotic short story...virginity. The teaching or introduction of a willing pupil to the arts of sex is very often found in all forms of erotica. There is a certain fascination about exploring virgin territory, so to speak. Every human being living today takes delight in being the first at one thing or another; being a virgin's (male or female) first partner is especially rewarding to the average individual.

This is the story of Phil, a young sailor of nineteen who is introduced into the twilight world of homosexuality. He finds himself to be an apt and willing student, and after mastering his lessons, he in turn becomes an experienced instructor.

ACT I

It had begun many years before. At first Phil had feared the hot-blooded giant and the strength that rose so unexpectedly between his legs to tantalize and plague him. But as time went by, he found the fascinating pleasure of this sturdy symbol of his increasing manhood. As his solid young body matured, he discovered the growing power of his masculinity, and more important, he discovered other young men only too willing to relieve these pressures that surged within him.

Phil was nineteen and had been in the Navy for almost a year. Gone were the days of high school track and swimming meets, gone the fumbling activities in the dark corners of the gym, gone the uncertainty of adolescence. Blond-haired, brown-eyed, slim but solidly muscled, Phil was ready to leave the innocence of youth for experience-trained manhood.

The hungry giant within him had been unsatisfied for many days when Jack suggested a moonlight swim at a secluded beach. Phil knew how Jack would relieve the long-contained desire—as he had once before—and he accepted the invitation.

The scene was set. The voice came willingly. The teacher was ready....

* * * * * * *

"Just like I said—nice and private, huh?" Jack was twenty-two or twenty-three and solidly proportioned. His hair was curly and dark, and his features were strong and mature. His white sailor's jacket clung to his powerful shoulders and narrowed slightly at his waist, and his trousers bound tightly to his solid legs, forming a heavy bulge at his crotch. "I told you I knew a good place."

"Yeah, it looks pretty good." Phil's face was cleanly hand-some, reflecting a mixture of youthful innocence and masculine maturity, and his body was trimly built. His deep brown eyes squinted as he looked out toward the ocean and moistened his narrow lips slowly. "I could sure go for a swim in the raw!"

"There'll be time for that later," Jack grinned, pulling up his jacket and rubbing one hand over the taut bronzed flesh covering his solid belly. "How about a drink?"

Jack picked up the pint bottle from the blanket spread on the sand, jerked off the cork and pressed it to his lips, swallowing hard. Then he passed it to Phil. As the younger sailor drank more slowly, more cautiously, Jack turned and pulled his jacket and T-shirt off over his head and sprawled on the blanket. Twisting on his back, he folded his arms under his head and watched the youth with a pleased smile. Then he stretched hard, rubbing one hand over the soft hair matting his full chest, and chuckled with pleasure.

"Want another?" Phil asked, stooping over and offering the bottle.

"You know what I want," Jack grinned, as he took the bottle again. "C'mon and relax."

As Jack drank, Phil stripped to the waist and joined him on the blanket. Phil's chest was full-curved and smooth, and his torso slimmed sharply to his narrow waist and trim hips. His flesh was evenly tanned and taut over smooth, rippling muscles. He was young and virile and athletic, like a blond statue come to life.

"How'd you ever find this beach, Jack?"

"A guy I met brought me down here." Jack passed the bottle to Phil. "We spent the night and nobody bothered us."

Lying side by side on their backs, the two young men talked softly, each enjoying the numbing sensation of the liquor and the mild night air against their flesh. At length Phil closed his eyes and relaxed, feeling the warmth of Jack's body almost touching his. Then Jack's hand was on the youth's chest, making lazy circular patterns over the smooth, tingling flesh, pausing to rub insistently over the wide, flat nipples at either side. Then the hand continued slowly over the taut stomach, the depression at the navel, the slight curve of the abdomen, to the stiff cloth of Phil's trousers. Jack's fingers pressed firmly down over the sailor's Pants to his crotch and dug deep into the cloth, testing the tempting flesh beneath. Then he drew his hand back and placed it on Phil's belly once more, this time forcing his fingers down inside the trousers, inside the shorts, deep into the warmth of the youth's groin—the crisp pubic hair, the firm, loose cock, the full, slippery balls.

Phil opened his eyes and grinned. He saw Jack gazing down at him keenly, the sparkling whiteness of his even smile, the solid curves of his muscular shoulders and arms, the fullness in his low-hanging trousers. He felt the fingers grip his genitals firmly, and then Jack was rolling over on top of him, pinning him down with his strong, young body.

"Take off your pants, Phil," Jack murmured excitedly. "Let's get going!"

Jack rolled away and sat up, unfastening his own trousers hastily and jerking them from his body. More slowly, Phil rose to his knees and began working his pants down from his hips and over his legs.

"You're too slow, buddy," Jack exclaimed, gripping Phil by the shoulders, and forcing him back on the blanket. For a moment he poised over the younger sailor, his nakedness edged with moonlight, his full, loose dick slowly growing stiff as the hot blood poured into its increasing length. His fingers gripped Phil's shorts, pulling them from his hips, pressing them down over his muscular thighs and legs, catching his trousers and yanking them from his ankles. "That's better!" His palms raced back and forth over Phil's genitals for a moment. "Shit, that feels good!" Then he threw himself, warm and naked and eager, on top of the waiting youth.

Phil felt the clean strength of Jack's body pressing down on him; he felt the powerfully muscled arms embracing him, forcing their bodies even closer together; he felt the exciting stimulation fill his groin as Jack's potent dick and balls rubbed against his own steadily; he felt the smoldering embers of desire within him burst into bright flames. A sharp cry broke from his throat.

"That's the way!" Jack whispered excitedly, pinning Phil on his back once more. He forced one hand between their bodies and gripped Phil's organs, rubbing them slowly. "Shit, that feels good. You sure are hung, buddy!"

Then Jack rose and sank back on his haunches, straddling Phil's legs. Smiling with anticipation, he let his eyes move slowly over the handsome, masculine figure lying before him. "Damn nice!" He placed his hands on Phil's legs and moved them slowly toward the youth's groin. His fingers slipped beneath Phil's large, loose balls, gripping them for a moment, then letting them fall free again. "I like a guy with big balls—the bigger the balls, the better the juice." His hand moved to the huge cock jutting thick and long and brittle-hard from Phil's crotch. His fingers wrapped around it and pulled slowly up and down its length. He rubbed his thumb lightly over the broad, flat head of the organ, feeling the dampness that had already begun to rise from within it. "Okay, buddy, I'm going to drain that bastard good!"

Jack dropped forward on top of Phil, his mouth pressed to the tanned flesh of his chest. His lips and tongue raced over the smooth, well-molded torso, nibbling, nuzzling, kissing. Waves of increasing excitement shot through Phil's body, and his breathing became sharp and strained as Jack's face moved closer and closer to his crotch and the climax waiting there. Then Jack's lips were pressed to the taut head of the throbbing pole, his tongue sweeping over it, his mouth consuming its potent length.

Phil groaned with delight as the rhythmic pressure began to gnaw at the dam holding back the flood within the youth. He closed his eyes, the undeniable demand for satisfaction growing within him, the passionate stimulation from Jack's experienced lips tearing at his groin. Every muscle of his body seemed to tense to the breaking point, and suddenly he sat up gripping Jack's head and forcing his cock to its ultimate in his throat.

"I'm gonna blast! I can't hold it! I'm gonna come!"

Jack reared up, wrapping his arms about Phil's thighs, and sliding his palms beneath his hips. He jerked the youth upward, taking the trembling cock completely into his mouth and feeling a shudder of ultimate excitement tear through the young sailor's body. Phil threw his head back and cried out hoarsely as his dick jerked uncontrollably and the first huge blast of thick liquid smashed into Jack's throat. Enveloped in a fury of passion, Phil felt burst after burst pour from his virile organ, and he fell back weakly, still forcing his organ into Jack's throat automatically. Jack continued to draw heavily on the trembling cock until the liquid flowed more and more slowly and finally stopped. Then he lowered the youth to the blanket again and slowly licked his tongue over the relaxing genitals.

Phil lay back, exhausted. He threw one arm over his eyes, and his full chest rose and fell sharply with his heavy breathing. Jack smiled and stretched out beside him.

"Damn good, huh?" the older sailor said quietly. "A lot better than back at the base when you couldn't strip or lie down or anything." He turned on his side and ran his fingertips lightly over Phil's smooth, sweat-damp chest. "I didn't know you'd like it so much or I'd have brought you down here the first time instead of messing around behind the barracks."

Phil pulled his arm from over his eyes and grinned at Jack. "Criminie, I never knew anything could feel so good!"

Jack chuckled. "Here's something else that feels plenty good." He grasped his own stiff rod firmly and pushed it toward Phil. "Ever play with a hot one?"

"Sure," Phil said positively, covering his inexperience. "In high school a couple of times. Sometimes we'd jack each other off." To prove his point, he reached over and gripped Jack's rigid dick with one hand firmly. He moved his fingers along its warm, potent length slowly, watching the ivory-smooth head gleam in the moonlight. "Gees, you've got a fine one!" he exclaimed in admiration. "Want me to pound it a little for you?"

"Bend over and get your lips around it, Phil. Like I did for you."

"I—I don't know—if I can," the young sailor stammered, staring at the tantalizing tool.

"Sure you can," Jack coaxed. "Try it—just a little."

Phil looked up at Jack for a short, hesitant moment, and then, sucking in a deep breath, he dropped his face to his friend's groin. Holding the potent meat upright in his hand, he pressed his lips to it. He let his tongue slip through to wash over the solid head, and then suddenly his lips opened to draw it into his mouth. He sucked hard for a moment, trying desperately to take it all in one swallow, and then he gagged. Coughing, he pulled back.

"I can't, Jack," he murmured. "I—can't."

"Try it again, Phil," Jack urged tensely. "You'll get the hang of it."

"I—I'm scared!"

"Here, I'll fix it up for you," Jack exclaimed eagerly. "Be ready to take it when it goes!"

Jack gripped his cock with one hand, holding his powerful balls with the other, and began to rub the rigid flesh rhythmically. Phil stared with fascination as the organ seemed to grow even longer and stiffer. Jack was breathing hard now, his body tense, his muscles jerking from time to time as the excitement increased within him.

"Get ready! Get down there, Phil!"

Drawn as though hypnotically, Phil crouched beside Jack, his eyes fixed on the hand racing rapidly up and down the inflamed organ. He saw the fingers of Jack's other hand working over his convulsing balls, and he felt a pounding excitement welling up inside his own virile young body.

"Now!" Jack gasped. "Take it! Drink it down!"

For an instant, Phil's world seemed to stand still. Before him he saw the handsome, naked youth lying on his back, legs spread, hips raised, rigid cock in his fingers. He heard Jack's panting breath, saw his tense expression, felt something of the powerful excitement that was overwhelming this naked man. The thick cock stood rigid from the nest of dark hair like an iron rod topped with a flange that gleamed with hardness, and a trace of this liquid bubbled up from the well in the center of it.

"Suck on it, Phil!"

Phil dropped his face to Jack's crotch, opening his mouth and accepting the quivering monster. His mind forgot the difficulty he had experienced before; now he thought only of consuming this trembling snake completely and drinking down its precious milk. He was only vaguely aware of the masculine body thrashing with passionate excitement, the hoarse breathing, the cries of pleasure. He felt only the wild stimulation of drawing the fiery pole into his throat, of rubbing his tongue over its throbbing length, of sucking deeply on its virility. Then in a confusion of passion and fury, of flesh and muscle, of darkness and light, the monster spit its first tremendous shower and followed it with another and another and another. Phil swallowed heavily, his lips dragging with an unending appetite at the source of the potent liquid.

"You're tearing me apart," Jack groaned weakly, falling back on the blanket.

Dazed, Phil felt an overwhelming reluctance fill him as the fierce giant in his throat began to weaken and grow soft. Numbly he drew away and sprawled beside Jack, caressing his sweat-streaked nakedness.

"Lemme rest a little," Jack murmured. "Then we'll do it again—both of us. I'll teach you to be the best damn cocksucker in the Navy before we're done!"

ACT II

Phil was young and virile. The giant had tormented him when he did not understand the power and pleasure it contained, but now it demanded more and more of the treatment that would fill it with fire, make it throb with strength, bring the liquid boiling up through its potent length. Jack had taught him this pleasure and the pleasure of accepting another man's satisfaction. Jack had introduced him to the inner world of dimly lit bars and dark streets, the eager-eyed young men, the places and means of meeting those who would gladly ease the giant's yearnings. Jack had been an able teacher and Phil a willing pupil.

Now a new teacher was ready with a new lesson....

* * * * * * *

"Stand right there, Phil—where I can see you."

Phil stood in the center of the darkened bedroom stripped to the waist. Enough light came through the windows so that he could make out every line of the naked man's body resting on the bed. Ted was twenty-nine, fairly tall and slim. His features were neat, friendly, and his body was sleekly muscled. He watched Phil with a keen gaze and gently stroked the relaxed meat hanging from his hair-filled crotch.

"C'mon, drop your pants, sailor."

Phil grinned at Ted and began to unfasten his trousers. Ted knew the score; Ted would show him a good time! He drew his pants off over his ankles and carefully folded them on the chair.

"You've got a beautiful build," Ted smiled. "You remind me of another sailor I knew. Only he was more innocent. I was the first one to brown him." He chuckled, massaging his dick steadily. "I bet you like being browned—you're nice and athletic."

Ted used a lot of phrases Phil didn't understand. "Sometimes," he shrugged noncommittally.

"You sailors are all alike," Ted chuckled. "I bet they bring you out with a piece of soap in the shower!" He moistened his lips with his tongue slowly. "Drop your shorts, Phil. I want to see all of it."

Phil paused for a moment, rubbing his fingers over the blond peach-fuzz on his chest; Jack said that hair showed he was a man. He let his eyes drop to the meat now rising firm and hard between Ted's fingers, and he felt a slight disappointment; he had thought there would be more. Then Phil ripped open his skivvies and pushed them down from his slim waist, roughing his fingers over his genitals. His cock dropped free and heavy, already anticipating the excitement to come, but not yet hard. Beneath it he could feel the strength of his handsome balls, and he smiled proudly.

"Beautiful!" Ted exclaimed softly. "I want to see it get hard! Bring it here and I'll play with it. I'll make that big bastard stand up and fire!"

Eagerly Phil approached the bed, and Ted sat up, reaching out to grasp the young sailor's dick and pull it toward his waiting mouth. Phil knelt straddling Ted's legs and felt the hungry lips close about his cock. Ted worked over the firm flesh with his tongue strongly until it grew solid and hard, and then he threw his head back and took it completely. Phil gripped the man's head, holding it in place firmly as he drove his organ downward into Ted's warm throat. Then, pleased at the ease with which Ted took it, Phil released him and drew away, settling back with a smile.

"Like that, Ted?"

"Shit, I'm as excited as a virgin in a daisy chain!" He lay back and held his arms up to Phil. "C'mere, honey." Phil fell forward on top of the naked man and they embraced, each pressing his body eagerly to the other's. "You magnificent bastard! I'm going to have you until you can't walk!" Ted's hands massaged Phil's muscle-ridged back strongly, working down slowly to his waist hips, his slim, tight-curved cheeks. "What an ass!" he sighed. "It's so tight, Phil—I can feel what it'll be like already!"

Eagerly, Ted forced Phil over on his back, falling on him heavily. Phil felt Ted's lips pressed against his own, and then Ted's hot tongue was driving like a spear-head into his mouth. The man's nakedness was pressing down on the youth, and Phil felt the growing excitement of the sensuous lips and the probing tongue. For the first time he was experiencing this act and finding it pleasant. Then Ted was pulling free.

"You like to French, don't you?" Ted murmured with a smile, falling on his back beside Phil.

"Yeah, I guess so," Phil grinned, running one hand over the man's mature body.

"What else do you like?"

Phil grasped Ted's cock and placed it upright against his own as he sprawled on top of him. "I dunno—what do you suggest?"

Ted wrapped his arms about the youth and chuckled. "I want to lay you on your back and French you all over. And every time you get hard, I want to take it." He ran his hands down over Phil's strong back. "I want to do you 'til you're worn out." He rubbed his palms over the young sailor's trim cheeks and felt them tense. "Then I want to brown you!" Ted smeared his fingers across his mouth quickly, covering them with spit and then working them deep into Phil's ass. "You've got a real tight one, but I know you can take it. I'll be nice and gentle—and you'll love it. C'mon, honey," he whispered, his voice husky with excitement, "let me screw you!"

Phil answered by dropping his full weight on the man, forcing their bodies even tighter together and searching out Ted's mouth with his lips. For the first time, he drove his tongue between the lips, duplicating Ted's quivering movements, then driving it into the warm, damp mouth fully. Then Ted jerked his head away.

"I can't wait!" he cried. "Take me! My God, take me!"

Infected with Ted's fury, Phil pressed even harder against the man's tense nakedness and found his mouth once more with his tongue. Ted struggled to free himself, and then a tremendous spasm shook through his body. An instant later, his cock trembled convulsively and then unloaded its liquid burden against Phil's belly. The climax ended as suddenly as it had begun, and Ted turned his head away, groaning.

"I wanted you to take it, Phil.... You lousy bastard, I wanted you to take it at least."

Phil rolled to his knees beside Ted, breathing hard. "I—I didn't think you'd go so fast."

Ted stared at the husky, naked youth and at the huge, rigid cock jutting from his groin as if demanding its satisfaction. "Fuck me, Phil," he murmured thickly, twisting away on his side. "Shove it to me all the way!"

Phil stared at the broad, smooth back and the full, relaxed cheeks. Numbly, he felt the angry desire within him and recognized this new source of relief. Quickly he bent forward and thrust his dick between the waiting cheeks.

"Oh no!" Ted groaned. "You're too big to take bare! Use some of my come to make it easier."

Phil reared back and ran his fingers over his belly, collecting the thick, cold liquid which Ted's climax had left there. Then he rubbed it over the head of his taut dick, feeling its stickiness drip down along the throbbing length of the organ. Breathing hard, he bent forward and slid his pole between Ted's cheeks.

"What a fucking machine!" Ted exclaimed. "I'll give it a ride to remember!" He reached back swiftly and seized the trembling organ, guiding it easily into his ass. "There, it's all yours!"

Phil felt the warm flesh open before the demanding head of his cock. He felt the new sensation, the excitement, the desire. Ted rose to his hands and knees, and Phil drove his cock forward into him.

"Screw it in, kid! Let me have all of it!"

The youth quickly found the speed, the position, the rhythm that pleased him most. This new act was wildly exciting, and he soon felt Ted's hips rising to meet the solid thrusts of his organ. Then the demands within him were overwhelming him, closing about him, cutting him off from reality. He did not hear Ted's cries of delight and pain and passion; he withdrew into a secret world where his mastery of this man was his total existence.

"Harder, Phil! Don't be afraid! Jam it to me!"

The rhythm became wild and uncontrollable. The flames in the youth's groin burned white-hot and demanding. And after what seemed like an eternity of fury, the throbbing flood burst its banks and boiled over. The sailor cried out and held the man tightly, driving the aching climax into him feverishly....

Phil lay on his back, lost in the darkened world of his satisfaction. He felt relaxed and strong and more alive than he had thought possible. Then he felt a damp towel rubbing over his flesh, washing his crotch carefully. Opening his eyes, he found Ted, still naked, bending over him, a pleased smile on his face.

"Gees, that was great, Ted!"

"You acted like you'd never done that before," Ted chuckled. "I guess a lot of guys are afraid to try a piece of meat as big as yours. I'm glad I'm not!"

"So am I!"

Ted straddled Phil's hips and bent low over him. "That isn't the only position, you know. I'll show you another as soon as you get it stiff again." He reached into Phil's crotch and gripped the heavy, relaxed cock. "Lovely!"

"Better take it easy," Phil smiled proudly. "That little beggar gets hungry real fast when you play with him."

"You're an athletic young stud," Ted sighed, rubbing his hands up over Phil's torso. "I want to have it every time you get hard—all night long." He lowered his body to the youth's and embraced him. "I put a jar of Vaseline on the table there. Use all you need, honey."

ACT III

The innocence of youth retreated farther into the past with each new experience.

Phil's body was maturing into solid, virile manhood, and with that manhood came a further intensity of the desire within him. Night after night he sought men who would worship before his magnificent young body and relieve the passions filling him. He went back to Ted often at first, but as time passed, he found other men eager to gain their own satisfaction in accepting a young sailor's demands. Phil was young and handsome, and his passion seemed almost unending. He knew what he liked, and he took what he wanted.

The student had learned many things from his teachers. Now he was to receive an unexpected lesson....

* * * * * * *

The three young sailors staggered down the street toward the lonely row of darkened barracks.

"Shit," Jack muttered, "everybody gets leave except us. Shit!"

"We oughta have a party," Phil said, stumbling against Jack and leaning on his shoulder heavily.

"You've already had a party," Bob grinned. "A real ball!"

Bob was several years older than Phil, with dark, wavy hair and narrow black eyes. He was solidly built and aggressively rugged. "I bet you had every guy there—except Jack and me."

"Bend over and I'll take care of you guys too!"

"No thanks!" Bob chuckled. "I'm not drunk enough to try that flag-pole of yours!"

Laughing, the three young men turned into one of the barracks and stood unsteadily together in the darkness.

"Nobody's home!" Phil exclaimed. "Let's go back to the party! There's a butch Marine I didn't get to screw!"

Phil turned toward the door again, but Bob caught him by the arm. "Hold it, kid. You've had enough partying. We'll have to give you a cold shower!"

Phil brushed the hand away, muttering, "I'm not drunk—I can give myself a shower!"

Grinning, Jack and Bob watched as Phil staggered down the barracks aisle to his bunk in the middle of the long row of empty cots. Sitting on the edge of the bed, he began unfastening his shoes laboriously.

"I'm surprised he can still walk," Jack chuckled. "I'd be beat if I'd done it as often and as hard as he did tonight. Did you see him with that little blond kid?"

"Some party!" Bob exclaimed, stretching hard and rubbing his palm over his crotch. "Yeah, it must have taken him fifteen minutes of solid pumping. That poor kid was out of his mind before Phil finally came!"

"I couldn't have taken a screwing like that." Jack glanced at Phil, who had gotten to his feet and started undressing. "I sure as hell wouldn't mind getting into him though."

"I figured you already had."

"Nope," Jack shrugged. "I doubt that anyone has."

"Bullshit!" Bob exclaimed softly. "You brought him out— you must have talked him into spreading his legs."

"I tried, but he's never let anybody do it." Jack grinned. "That guy he was with at the party tonight told me he was going to brown Phil if it was the last thing he did—and you saw who ended up getting fucked!"

"That's no lie!" Bob gripped the heavy organs within the crotch of his trousers. "I started to drip just watching. Criminie, what control!" He glanced down the barracks to where Phil stood stripped to his shorts, and he felt his heavy cock throb with life. "Damnit, that ass makes me hot! It's built for screwing!"

"Let me know if you make the grade," Jack chuckled. "But I'll bet he gets you instead." He stretched and yawned. "I'm going to hit the sack. There's a real beautiful young thing who just moved into my barracks and I think he'll go for it now that no one else is there."

Bob sat on his bunk and began to undress as Jack left. Further down the room he saw Phil throw a towel over his shoulder and start toward the shower room. The youth's back rippled with trim muscles and his tight cheeks rose and fell sharply with his easy gait. Bob thought about how hot he was and how drunk Phil was and how satisfying Phil's ass would be.

Bob leapt to his feet and jerked his jacket and T-shirt over his head, rubbing one hand over the solid curves of his hair-matted chest. Then he dropped his shorts and trousers, pausing to finger his heavy genitals proudly.

"I know what you need," he murmured, staring down at his sturdy cock. "And he's got it!" He picked up his shaving kit and towel and started toward the shower room. "Let's get it!"

Phil was standing under a shower spray, rubbing a bar of soap aimlessly over his nakedness, as Bob entered.

"Pretty drunk, huh?" Bob asked with a grin.

"Who's drunk?" Phil demanded, stumbling from under the water.

"You are, kid." Bob took the soap from Phil's hand. "Turn around and I'll wash your back."

Bob began working the soapy lather over Phil's bronzed back in widening circles, and as his hands slid down over the smooth flesh, he stepped closer, pausing occasionally to quickly wipe a handful of foam over his own stiffening dick. Then his palms cupped over Phil's sleek, trim cheeks, and he sucked in a sharp breath as his fingers slipped deep between them. Phil stood motionless, his legs slightly spread, only vaguely aware of what Bob was doing.

Bob's cock was rigid and hard now, and suddenly he thrust it between Phil's cheeks. The young sailor jerked back in surprise, and Bob's organ slipped on forward between his legs.

"Hey, what's this?" Phil asked with mock curiosity, reaching down beneath his balls to grasp the potent dick. "A real hot one, huh?" He rubbed his thumb over the taut, soap-covered head, watching the throbbing meat quiver. "Want me to palm it off?"

"I know something better," Bob murmured tensely, drawing his rigid cock back and wiping his well-lathered hand over its turgid length once more. "Relax, Phil." Carefully he guided the head of his cock between Phil's cheeks and then thrust his hips forward hard, feeling the warm tightness of the youth's virgin ass about it. "There!"

For a moment the two men stood stationary, and then Phil stiffened with a gasp. "Hey!"

"C'mon, Phil, relax! I'll be real gentle! You'll like it!"

"Cut it out," Phil exclaimed thickly, starting to pull away.

"Let it in, Phil!" Bob wrapped his arms about the youth's waist, forcing his cock brutally against the resistance. "Bend over a little and it'll slip right in. It won't hurt."

"Cut it out!" Phil repeated, straining to get free of the arms holding him, the body pressing against his back, the giant jabbing between his cheeks.

Wildly, Bob forced the rigid organ into Phil again and again, trying to pierce the wall set up against him. "I gotta have it, Phil! I gotta have it!"

"Lemme go!" Phil's body was tense, every muscle straining. "Lemme go!"

"I can't stop now!" Bob cried. "It'll only take a minute! Just let it in a little way!" His hands slipped down and cupped over Phil's genitals. "Let me fuck you—just a little—and I'll let you have me any way you want."

"Cut it out, you sonofabitch!" Phil exploded, jabbing his

elbow into the pit of Bob's stomach and breaking free. "Get away from me!"

Bob leaned back against the wall of the shower room, expecting his cock to spew its boiling load onto the floor. Numbly he watched Phil duck under the shower again. "Please, Phil," he begged softly, "don't leave me like this. Look, it's all set to pop! C'mon, Phil!"

Dazed, Phil let the water sluice down over his face and body, washing the soapy lather from his nakedness, and then he staggered into the head to dry off. Helpless, Bob watched him work the towel over his body haphazardly and then stumble through the door to the barracks.

Bob sucked in a deep breath. His husky body was still covered with soap from Phil's back and his cock hung down thick and full over his heavy balls, still warm with the sensations of the climax it had almost reached. Bob ran his hand down over his belly and grasped his meat, wrapping his fingers around it and massaging its sturdy length.

"It'd only take a little to get you stiff again and make you shoot," he muttered, staring at the strong organ. Then he dropped it. "Hell, Jack might be back—or something!"

Bob took his time showering and drying off carefully. At last he wrapped his towel about his hips, picked up his shaving kit and went into the barracks.

A beam of light from the streetlamp outside filtered through a window and fell across Phil's bunk. The youth lay on his stomach, his arms folded under his head, breathing deeply with drunken sleep. Bob paused to watch the handsome, relaxed features, the sleek blond hair, the smooth tanned flesh taut over the heavy muscles of the shoulders and arms. His eyes followed down noting how the blankets clung to the dip in the small of the youth's back and then rose sharply over the smooth-rounded curves of his ass. Bob ran his tongue over his lips and thought of the moments in the shower when the conquest was almost his, and he felt the familiar tenseness of desire come alive in his crotch once more. Then he bent over the bed and gripped the youth's shoulder.

"Asleep, Phil?" The youth did not move, and a pleased grin curled Bob's lips. His hand slipped from the youth's shoulder and gripped the blanket, pulling it down slowly to the foot of the bed. Phil's handsome body lay naked and relaxed, and Bob let his hands move over it gently, pausing to probe between the trim cheek with his fingers. "Passed out, huh?" Slowly Bob spread Phil's legs apart. "Maybe you'll wake up in time for the fun!" The sleeping sailor did not move.

Bob straightened and ran his hands over the black hair matting his burly chest. Then he jerked the towel from his waist. His cock hung down firm but not yet hard between his legs, and he raised it with one hand as he grasped his balls with the other. His nuts were loose and large and slippery, and he held them tightly, feeling the sensuous pain start to fill his groin. His dick stiffened quickly, the wide, flat head growing tense and hard as steel. He dropped his organs, arched his back and stretched proudly, his cock jutting out from his crotch potent and strong.

Then Bob dumped the contents of his shaving kit on the empty cot beside Phil's and picked out the small tube of lubricant. Hastily he smeared some on his fingers and then bent over Phil, working these fingers between the sleeping youth's cheeks carefully. He added more and more of the greasy ointment until he had the passage well-oiled and felt it relax.

"That's the way, baby," Bob muttered. "Now you'll take it nice and easy." He gripped his huge, rigid cock and slowly applied a light coat of lubricant to the taut head, grinning at it. "Take it easy, old man. There's no rush this time!" He knelt on the bed between Phil's muscular thighs. "This is the way I've wanted you for a long time, Phil!"

Bob gripped Phil's sturdy cheeks, spreading them wide, and bent forward, carefully slipping his mighty cock between them. Deeper and deeper the organ went, and Bob caught up a deep breath of pleasure.

"There, the bulldozer's opened the trail and the rest'll go easy. Real easy!"

The youth stirred and groaned. Through a veil of drink and sleep, Phil felt the man's body pressing down on him, the fingers digging into the solid muscles of his arms, the huge organ easing its way deep into his helpless form. He felt numb, unable to fight or call for help or beg for an end to it. Who was this man using him? It was as though he was a bystander, watching from a distance. A man he couldn't see was fucking a drunken youth. A handsome young sailor naked on his belly—empty barracks—being fucked by—? And he was that sailor!

"Don't—please!" Phil heard his voice come as though from another throat. "I can't take it!"

"You've already got it, baby," Bob said hoarsely, forcing his cock as deep as it would go. "I told you it'd be easy. Grit your teeth and hang on!"

Bob drew his hips back until the head of his cock almost slipped from Phil's tight asshole. Then he drove it forward again, drew it back, thrust it forward. Phil felt the fury, the passion, the body smashing down on him, pinning him to the firm mattress; he heard the man's panting breath, the groans of desire; he saw the world spin before his eyes, flames licking at his brain, brilliant colors bursting in the darkness that closed about him. From far off, Phil heard a voice, choked, straining, begging for it to stop, and he realized vaguely that it was his own voice.

"All the way, baby!" Bob cried, oblivious of Phil's begging. "Give it to me!" He wrapped his arms about Phil's waist, jerking the youth's hips high into the air and driving his trembling dick into the hot, slippery ass for the final time. "Take it, goddamnit—take it!"

Then it was over. Bob lay heavily on top of Phil, breathing hard, sweat-beads forming between his shoulder blades and dripping down his back. At last, his heart ceased its mad pounding, his breathing slowed to normal, his cock softened between the young sailor's cheeks.

"That's okay, kid," he said gently, rubbing his hands over Phil's shoulders and arms. "We'll just lie here like this for a little while. Lie here like this with my dong still inside you. And when it gets hard again, I'll roll you over on your back and let you try it that way. And after that...." He sighed. "You'll get the full treatment tonight, Phil!"

EPILOGUE

The lessons had been learned, each in its own time. Hesitantly at first, then with more and more confidence, the youth had put his training to use, taking what he wanted, offering what he wished. Slowly he had learned what he liked and what he didn't like, how to get what he wanted to get and not give what he didn't want to give. Where he had once feared the demanding giant at his groin, now he felt its virile strength proudly, knowing the many forms of satisfaction it could give him.

And so youth gave way to manhood, and student became teacher....

* * * * * *

Phil stood on the beach stripped to the waist, tight-binding Levi's hanging low on his hips. The night was dark but he could see the restless surf wash against the sand in endless motion. He rubbed one hand over the soft blond hair curling over his broad full chest, and he grinned, thinking of the first time he had come here....

That was three years ago, and he had been young and innocent as he had lain naked on the blanket and allowed Jack to drink down the fire that burned so hotly between his legs. He chuckled softly as he thought of his first fumbling attempts to give Jack the same satisfaction that night, and of the other men on whom he had practiced and become proficient. He thought of the delights in discovering new methods, new experiences with each new partner. He remembered warmly the words of praise for his handsome face, his powerful body, his massive genitals. And he smiled as he thought how willing these men had been to do whatever he wanted.

Ted had been willing. He had talked rough and demanding, but he had given himself to Phil in a way that the sailor had not then experienced before. With that experience came an irresistible need for repeating it—again and again—with many men, willing and unwilling.

Phil himself had been unwilling when Bob first forced him into accepting this same act. But here too, he had learned and learned well.

Phil sucked in a deep breath. He was no longer the slim, lithe youth with innocent eyes, smooth chest and loins aching for unknown experiences. His features had grown strong, handsome, mature, and his body was solidly muscled and ruggedly developed. Proudly he let one hand find the bulging crotch of his Levi's and feel the powerful warmth beneath the coarse cloth. He'd come a long way in three years!

Phil turned and sauntered slowly to the large blanket spread on the sand. Walt, a husky sailor several years younger than Phil, lay there on his back. Shirtless, a light growth of dark hair shadowed his high-curved chest and made a soft trail down over his belly, disappearing beneath his Levi's. His black hair was short-cut, his features neat and youthful, and he showed his even, white teeth as he smiled at Phil.

"Want another round, Phil?" he asked, offering the half-empty pint bottle.

Phil grunted and drank deeply. Then he returned the bottle to the youth and fell on the blanket beside him. "Good beach, huh? Good and private."

"Great! Hey, thanks for loaning me these civvies. I haven't been out of uniform since I joined up last fall!"

Phil grinned. "You're just getting started, and I'm almost out. Two weeks to go!"

"Gees!" Walt rolled on his side toward Phil. "Are you going to miss the Navy?"

"I dunno. I've learned a lot in the last four years." He smiled at the athletic young sailor beside him. "You'll learn a lot too."

Walt took another deep swallow from the bottle and lay back, staring into the darkness overhead. "You're a good guy, Phil. I'm going to miss you."

Phil looked down at the half-naked youth and smiled. The night air was invigorating and he had drunk enough to feel pleasantly relaxed, and the young sailor was quite attractive. "You're a good guy too, Walt." With seeming carelessness, he placed one hand on the boy's firm warm chest, letting his fingers caress the soft, dark hair and the wide, flat nipples. "You look pretty rugged, too." His hand moved down over the taut, hard stomach. "You sure fill those Levi's!" Phil placed his hand firmly on Walt's crotch, feeling the solid bulge beneath his fingers. "Not much room for growth, huh?" He dug his fingers into the warm flesh beneath the cloth and felt the rising potency.

Walt laughed softly, excitement tinged with nervousness. "Take it easy, Phil. You'll get it hard doing that!"

"I'm not worried," Phil murmured with pleasure as he felt the youth's cock stretch down along his thigh beneath his Levi's. "I'll show you how to take care of it."

"You mean like palming it off?" Walt asked with a shy grin. "Hell, I already know about that!"

"I know something lots better." Gently, insistently, Phil worked his fingers between the metal buttons along the trousers' fly. He knew Walt had not worn shorts tonight—he'd talked him into that himself—and now his fingers touched the warm, bare flesh and the crisp pubic hairs. After a moment, he began to unfasten the buttons. "Just lie back and relax, buddy."

"Hey!" Walt moved to cover his fly with his hand, then pulled it away slowly as he felt his trousers laid open and his genitals pulled free. He closed his eyes as Phil's fingers grasped his balls, investigating their firm slipperiness gently, and then closed about his thick, rigid cock, massaging it slowly, steadily. "Criminie, Phil!" he breathed.

Phil stared down at the hearty piece of meat in his hand, rising stiff and straight like a virile young soldier snapping to attention. He felt the growing surge of excitement between his own legs, and he dropped his mouth to the tense organ waiting for him.

Walt gave a stifled cry of surprise as the strong lips found his dick. Then the moist tongue was rubbing over it hotly and his whole body reacted to the fire it brought. Phil consumed the rigid cock completely, drawing it deep into his throat and urging its climax steadily. His hands caressed the youth's hips, his abdomen, his chest, and then Phil drew back and sat up suddenly. Breathing hard with excitement, he grasped Walt's Levi's and tore them down off his legs. Now the sailor lay before him, young and virile and athletic. And ready!

Walt twisted about on the blanket, frantic with excitement as Phil's lips found his throbbing cock once more, dragging from its depths the furious explosion of thick, creamy liquid at last.

Phil heard the youth's breathless exclamations of satisfied pleasure. He sat back on his haunches and studied the rugged, naked sailor lying before him, and he thought of that night so long ago when he had lain on this same beach for the first time. He dropped one hand to the crotch of his Levi's and felt the pulsating hardness of his own dick. Then he ripped open his trousers and squirmed from them, kneeling across the youth on the blanket.

Walt looked up with surprise and, perhaps, fear—fear of the unknown. Poised over him was his friend Phil, naked, powerfully athletic, maturely built. From Phil's crotch rose the huge, thick, rigid organ, its inflamed potency unquestionable. He saw Phil grasp this massive pole and press it toward him.

"Here, Walt, try it a little."

Numbly, Walt saw the instrument come closer and closer to his face, and then he was raising his head to press his lips to the hard, throbbing head, tasting the thin, watery liquid already dripping from it, and finally accepting its full length.

"That's the way!" Phil sighed, running his fingers over Walt's short-clipped hair. "Suck it down." He smiled at the surprising ease with which Walt was handling this new experience, and he thought of all the other acts this youth could be taught. "Take it easy, Walt. We've got two weeks!"

CHAPTER TWO
WELL, I'LL BE A HORSE'S ASS

This second example of the erotic story is unique among such efforts. In the first place, it touches upon bestiality, not terribly common in erotica. Moreover, it has a whimsical quality that is also uncommon. But most unusual of all is its mythological subject matter; with rare exceptions, erotic tales of this sort lean toward the present and an exaggerated "realism". But here we find references to Zeus and his wife Hera, to Mars and Apollo and Ganymede and numerous other residents of Olympus. We have magic spells no less, in the grand tradition of Snow White and associates.

Also interesting is another peculiarity—numerous authorities on homosexuality have asserted that the urge for fellatio springs directly from the breast sucking of infancy. Some critics disagree, but in this tale we have an excellent illustration of such a theory, as Hercules refers frequently to the penis he is sucking as a "tit". It is through just such revelations that erotica enables us to better understand the sexual workings of the mind.

* * * * * * *

Hercules the Hero had just finished cleaning the Augean Stables and was bathing in the river, washing off the smelly shit of the animals, when he heard a whinnying sound behind him. Turning, he discovered a Centaur with the sleek body of a horse and the torso of a rugged young man with an extremely handsome, but very unhappy face. As at the sight of any gorgeous man, Hercules felt a tingling sweetness in the dangle of his huge penis, especially as he could not help noticing the stallion-size of the prick that swung heavily between the Centaur's legs as the creature reared excitedly.

Herc had frequently frolicked with the Centaurs, but this was one he had never seen before, and the sadness of the lovely face intrigued him strangely. "Who in the name of Hades are you?" asked the muscle-man, "and what seems to be your trouble?"

"I am named Equesto," the Centaur said, "and I have been watching you and I believe you are the only one who can help me!"

Never one to turn down a guy in trouble, Hercules begged Equesto to elucidate. "Well," said Equesto, "my father was playing around with my mother...but they weren't married, you see! He was hitched to another woman, but the old boy likes a variety of cunts, and, well...Ma likes a variety of dicks. He had a nice one, you know, but she just happened to remark as she played with it, that she'd like sometime to really be screwed by a real stud of a man. Quick as a flash the guy changes himself into a horse...a stallion, and puts the ole yard-arm to her. He really fucked the pure piss out of her pussy! (Hercules gasped, but remained silent as Equesto went on.) Naturally he knocked her up with that tool that drove in clear up to her belly...but his wife caught them while he was still frigging the hell out of her juicy slit, and she said that I would be born half-man, half-horse, as you can see, I am!"

"Is your father, by any chance, Zeus, the King of the gods?" Hercules asked then.

"Why, yes!" Equesto replied.

"Then, old fellow," Herc said, slipping an arm affectionately about the Centaur's shoulder, and loving the feel of rippling muscle against his flesh that sent a helpless stiffness pulsing into his big peter, "we're half-brothers because Zeus is my dad, too!"

"What?" Equesto exclaimed, astounded.

"Let's face it, boy, our old man is a fuckin' fool!" Hercules grinned. "He was diddling around my old lady's crack too, and *she* just happened to remark she'd like just once to be jazzed by a real bull. Yep, just like that he changed into a big rutting bull and he creamed her with that huge cock and loaded balls until the juice was pouring out of her and she was pleading for mercy! Fortunately his real wife didn't catch them, so I was born okay...but I got those big balls and peter from Pa!" He held up his meat in his hands, perhaps fondling it a bit too much and that old tool was beginning to stick out stiffly.

Equesto eyed the herculean (if you excuse the expression) prick, with a far from casual gaze. "Beautiful! Just beautiful!" he said, reverently.

"You're kinda hung, too!" Hercules said admiringly, because the Centaur was having a little trouble between his legs also!

"Which brings me to my problem, Herky!" Equesto said, as his huge penis lifted heavily. "It's sex!"

At the strong man's quizzical look, the Centaur went on, "Well, as you can see," he said, indicating his enormous cock which hung on a throbbing horizontal by now, "my damn tool is just too far removed to reach comfortably with my hands, so I can't even jack myself off! As far as women are concerned I despise them and wouldn't touch one of the bitches, even if I could. What I'd really like to do is knock it off with another guy, but every man I've propositioned has turned white as a sheet, gasped, and high-tailed it out of there! So I've got a constant case of the hots, and who wants to relieve his nuts just in 'Wet Dreams?' Then I saw you, Herky, never realizing you were my brother...but so much the better, because I believe you can help me if you will!"

Hercules' eyes misted with tears of sympathy for his brother's predicament. He knew what it was to have the yen...real bad... but he had never had any trouble finding guys to fuck or suck. Most men were happy to oblige a fellow with a big juicy prick... if he was a man! But who ever heard of screwing around with a horse? "You're damn right I'll help you, buddy!" the muscular youth said, trying to figure out how to tackle this problem, and eager to get to it, because Equesto's magnificent penis made his mouth water. His own prick wasn't doing too bad either, hard and twitchy with delicious little tingles trickling up from his big balls, and Equesto fondling it with his hand, wasn't making it any easier! "Why don't you try sitting down for a start," Hercules suggested, trying to help his brother as he wriggled and slid about awkwardly until he was resting on his butt, with his cumbersome hind legs spraddled ungracefully. But who the heck was thinking of grace with that massive peter sticking up like a young tree-trunk, jerking exquisitely with anticipation? Gods! That dick must have been well over twelve inches long and every bit of three inches thick, and the utter stiffness had skinned back the glans so that it thrust out burstingly like an enormous purplish plum, sleek with juices.

"Let's see!" Herc said, more or less to himself, as he slid down beside his brother, his own pecker reaching out so stiffly it ached.

Equesto might have been driven out of his fucking mind by its beauty, if he hadn't been so concerned just then with his own peter. He couldn't help sobbing out happily as Hercules' fingers curled about his big hunk of meat and pumped it tenderly. "Ooooh," he moaned, "that feels so good! That feels so good!"

And it was true! The knowing touch of an expert hand *can* send sweet shivers of sensation tingling through a guy's nuts! Equesto leaned back, quivering with an indescribable delight, sighing with happiness in this newly found pleasure of those stroking fingers. And it gave Hercules a particular thrill in his own testicles to watch the shuddering, whimpering ecstasy of his brother over such unimportant stimulation. The muscle builder had known far more exquisite refinements of genital manipulation he had picked up in his travels, and especially in his voyage with the Argonauts and Jason in the search for the Golden Fleece. Believe me, those guys didn't just pull at oars! And Herc intended to share some of that delicious knowledge with this poor victim of Hera's bitchery!

The Centaur was lolling back, steeping his senses in that flickering digital dallying between his wide, wavering hind legs, as his brother worked the swollen stud's shaft up and down between his fingers, sometimes dragging the thin foreskin down fiercely so that the glands popped up like a fat succulent egg of enormous size, the lip of it gaping and oozing wetly with the slimy clear secretion of desire.

Hercules gazed at the swollen, glistening bulb hungrily. He had blown some pretty big boogers in his time. He had often said that Jason had the largest peter in the world (modestly, of course, excluding himself!) But this joy-job put even the gorgeous Jason to shame! And now, hungry to taste it on his tongue, he leaned over quickly, sinking his lecherous liquid lips down over the tremendous tit. Seized with the sudden sucking sensation that sent darts of stinging sweetness streaking through his balls and belly, Equesto squealed out deliriously, retching under the strong grip of his brawny brother. If Here's mouth had been free, he would have squealed too, for this was the best tasting penis he had ever eaten...a marvelously ripe animal flavor in the warm, hard, throbbing meat, the richly salty jets of piss that squirted generously over his taste-buds with each dredging drag of his lips up the succulent nipple. Already he had forgotten Equesto as his fingers laced demandingly about the Centaur's swollen root and he lugged great nursing sucks off the tool between his twisting lips....

"Oh, shit, Herky," Equesto sobbed, "I just can't take this any longer laying down!" His brother did not even stop in his munching, muttering feast on that luscious peter to answer, and as the Centaur struggled clumsily to his feet deliciously incapacitated by those delirious lips as by his ungainly build, Hercules did not lose a single suck on that tasty tit.

Rearing and resting his front hoofs on a tree trunk, the happy half-man, half-horse looked down on the frantically bobbing head of his princely brother, hardly able to believe that anything could feel so thrillingly good as the rich, velvety slide of those lips, massaging his throbbing meat rhythmically. "Ooo baby," he wept blissfully, "I never knew anything could be so beautiful! Oh, I saw Ganymede blowing Zeus one time...the way the old man retched back, all out of control, sobbing hysterically as the kid tapped his nuts with his lips...but I never knew it could be this utterly beautiful!"

Well, Hercules knew how ole Zeus had felt! One time he had waggled his prick at that cute kid, Ganymede, and they had slipped off behind some rocks and the boy had wrapped those lips around Herc's prong and had sucked the strong man down to his knees, jerking and crying out with a babbling idiocy as it felt like his big balls were melting off with sensation and being drunk down the lad's greedy throat along with his cum. Zeus hadn't kidnapped that boy from his parents for nothing... that boy knew how to eat a peter, and loved that hot creamy cum more than all the ambrosia on Olympus! There wasn't a male god who hadn't been sucked clean out of his mind by that marvelous child!

But Hercules hadn't known there was a dick anywhere as delicious as this one! It had a taste in its long, thick, glistening stem that tantalized his tongue insanely. Hanging on Equesto's quivering haunches, the muscular gay-boy twisted and turned his lips up and down on the nozzle trying to capture the furtive flavor that drove him wild with desire! Mmmm, it was so good! Maybe it was in the glans! He hung on the huge spastic shaft that protruded brown and muscular from the hairy root between those silky flanks, as he nibbled and sucked and licked all about the enormous bulb, making Equesto buck convulsively and squeal hysterically. Or maybe it was those huge, dangling balls! He ducked down and licked the tremendous hairy eggs in their bag, nursing each orb in the streaming baths of his mouth's saliva, making the Centaur cry like a baby! Maybe it was the rich, ripe horsey odor between those glossy haunches that sheltered his meaty genitals and gave them that added deliciousness of flavor! He nuzzled into the warm moist haven between Equesto's hind legs, sniffing about the balls, licking the sleek silky skin...a fragrance to make one drunk with lust!

The trembling Centaur was whinnying giddily, beside himself, his huge cock jerking joyously, when Hercules decided, No! It was that delicious dick and nothing else.... Equesto squealed hysterically as Hercules' lips suddenly sank back down over the hugely throbbing cock. The unexpected sucking attack of that ravenous mouth sent thrills shooting like streaks of delicious lightening through his pendulous balls and quivering flanks. He was so clutched with the pleasure he was not even aware that he farted with a helpless explosiveness! "Oooh shit, baby," he whimpered, "I didn't know anything could feel so good! Now I understand why the old man jumped around like a crazy snake while that kid was eating him! Oh Herky, I don't know if I can stand it or not!"

But his muscled brother knew he would...he hadn't met a guy yet who yelled "Stop!" before he shot his wad. And anyway, Hercules knew that he, himself, wouldn't stop even if his horsey partner begged him to, because this was one of the sweetest tasting tits he had ever nursed on. Mmmm, it was just so delicious!

Resting on his hands and haunches for better leverage, he ate that dick like there'd never be another, taking long pulling sucks, rolling the bulb lingeringly in the fluid feast of his lips before swooping down on it again, with a greedy sob, to suck up the stem again. The Centaur shivered violently with each swallowing swabbing suck, clear down to the root, and moaned dementedly with each slow, savoring suck back up to the head where that rolling, spit-lubricated massage on just the bulb made him squeal again, with punctuating farts. "Oooh man! Ooooh shit, man!" he sobbed. "It's so good! It's so beautiful! Oh Herky, I can't stand it! My balls feel so good!"

But Hercules was eating for cum, now! His mouth, though a sea of saliva, was parched for that sweet creamy boy-honey! He rocked back and forth furiously, dredging, devouring that delicious dick with thick guttural grunting sounds of hungry pleading. His lips smacked and belched in the ravenous attack, employing every thrilling twist and slide to provoke the warm, milky lava to eruption from Equesto's swinging testicles. And from the wild, incoherent whimpering sounds dripping from the Centaur's lips, he knew he'd get that fountain soon!

And then Equesto was babbling like an idiot, "Oh, god, Herky, it's too much...I'm going to shit...I'm going to faint...it's good...it's good...my balls! Oh shit, I'm coming...I'm coming!" He retched convulsively in a nausea of dizzying sensations that shot his load like a spurting spigot into his brother's rabid mouth. Rich, buttery cream filled Hercules' mouth in a flood, and his tongue, bathed in the milky sweetness, tasted the heavenly healthy goodness that is solely male! With a gluttonous grunt he swallowed that massive tool to its root and drank the goop with greedy gulps, while the Centaur jerked and sobbed deliriously in the pure discovery of heaven!

But at last the soaring climax flowed away, leaving Equesto feeling drained but deliciously content, still reared against the tree as his brother nursed away the last dewy dribbles from the lip of his softening peter. Hercules lipped and lapped with a lingering tenderness about the bulbous head, still savoring the ambrosial cum he had drunk from its gushing tip. But when he released the thickened tit and it dangled once more between his hind legs, the Centaur with a blissful sigh dropped his front hoofs to the ground. "Man, that was sweet!" he said happily.

But the muscled son of Zeus was inspired now, and he moved behind Equesto and dropping to his knees he lifted the dark, plumy tail that twitched back and forth over the glossy rump, to feed his eyes on the fat, brown puckered hole of the Centaur's ass. "What are you up to now, Herky?" the horse-man asked with giddy eagerness, feeling anticipatory tingles in his shit.

"I'm going to fuck your ass, baby brother!" Hercules told him, never taking his eyes away from that pooching pit that was contracting and gaping like a greedy mouth already. It looked moist, richly, gooily snug, like delicious molasses, and good enough to eat. It prompted the strong youth to add, "But first I'm going to eat you out good so you'll be able to take my prong without too much trouble! Here, grab this damn tail of yours and hold it up out of the way so I can eat you easier!"

Equesto whinnied with nervous ecstasy, glancing down to note the huge distension on Herky's cock. My god, it was big enough to choke a horse! The thought, apropos as it was, made the Centaur giggle and relax. "You remember the other day when it became rather dark?" he asked. "Well, the reason was that Mars had taken Apollo into a nearby grotto and was fucking the piss out of his ass...from the rear. He had that cute golden blond laid over on a mossy rock putting his peter into him like a crazy pump...it looked good and it must have felt good the way Apollo kept squealing and Mars kept sobbing!"

Hercules knew there was no need to reassure his brother. He'd find out soon enough that a big dick up his ass was far sweeter than he could have imagined. Instead, holding to Equesto's shanks as the Centaur drew back his tail, Hercules ducked down his handsome head, sniffing the shitty fragrance of the meaty hole, and then licked it, thrusting his tongue into the pitted opening, and rimmed it. His brother squealed happily, feeling little tingles darting through his bowels at this intimate caress, and then sobbing with sheer delight as the strong man glued his lips about the anus and began sucking it voraciously and eating into it with a greediness that plunged his feasting lips deep into the elastic opening, lubricating and loosening it for the moment when his tool would pierce it on its deep thrust....

When Hercules had Equesto's rectum thoroughly soupied and the Centaur was sighing contentedly and ready for anything, the good-looking, muscular youth stood up. He saw right away that it would be impossible to connect with the asshole without standing uncomfortably on tip-toes. "Hades!" he exclaimed angrily, trying in vain to stick it in anyway.

"What's the matter, Herky?" Equesto asked nervously.

But ingenuity and tingling desire had already discovered a solution, and the horseman squealed with surprised fear as Herc suddenly seized the backs of the Centaur's haunches and lifted his hoofs off the ground, and then deftly settled the pooching, puckering anus squarely on the bulbous tip of his stiffly erected penis. And even before his brother could cry out, he loosened the grip enough to allow the heavy weight of the horsey body to sink down, driving his dick deliciously deep into Equesto's shithole.

The Centaur screamed out with a delirious delight, feeling the thick, long living tool drilling far up into his bowels. Actually it did not hurt in the least, for horses have larger crap-holes than men, so it took Hercules' stallion-shaft easily. But, oh, the indescribable pleasure of feeling that piercing plunge, straight to the pit of passion. The long lunge of life itself communicated a thrilling tingle to every vital nerve-end of sensation. And for Hercules, who had screwed Argonaut asses until he had thought he had experienced every turd-hole thrill possible, it was the ball-melting discovery of a New Olympus! Even the asshole of Mercury which had introduced the stripling strong-boy to the first fun of fucking, causing the red-faced youth to helplessly shit joy, lost its aura of the "finest" sucking short of his half-brother. It was like slipping his peter into the ravenous relish of a mouth that was lecherous, laving lips, possessing every inch of dick as it went in with a liquid lusciousness of love!

As the feeling raced to his balls, threatening to release his wad if his dick drank the depths of Equesto's ass with one total thrust, Hercules, squealing in concert with his partner, renewed his grip on the Centaur's haunches to arrest the downward drive of that willing asshole, even pulling up Equesto's butt a bit as he did so, experiencing an unexpected bit of elusive electricity. He remembered now how the imaginative Mercury on that first excursion into Ecstasy had instructed him to place his strong hands under the god's lithe, light legs and move him up and down quickly, shallowly on his prick as they pranced about in a passionate polka. Hercules had howled with rapture and then helplessly squirted the shit like bullets even as he squirted his youthful cum into the giggling Mercury's belly! Now he moved Equesto's ass up and down on his tool while they both squealed like idiots, but he was older and more experienced now, and though it churned his shit with sensation, he kept a tight asshole!

But Equesto was no Mercury for weight, though he had a dreamier, creamier ass, and Herky's arms began to tire, and even the Centaur's front legs were wearying of their extra strain. So Hercules said, as he let his brother's back hoofs rest on the ground, thereby losing almost the total touch of their lovely union, "Let's fix you in a more restful position." The muscled youth was already rolling the Centaur over on his back. Equesto knew he was in the hands of an expert and moved willingly, just anxious to get that dick back deep in his butt, which was glowing with good feeling already. "Draw your legs way back," Herky said as he got on his knees waddling in with his big slimy peter leveled, to sink it in again, "because I'm going to fuck the shit out of your ass, baby!"

The promise thrilled the Centaur with a stabbing sweetness in the pit of his pendulous nuts and as he drew his legs back, a hugeness of hardness surged into his big meaty peter, and it twitched vigorously with anticipation. The sight of this massive male-tit, with its bulby glans fully peeled and bursting with juices, and the swollen bloated balls in their deep, loose bag hanging back against the thick, throbbing shaft, and down there between the spread buttocks just underneath the plumy switch of the Centaur's tail, that fat, brown, greedy rectum frothy already with fucking juices, brought as vigorous a vitality to Hercules' prick, extending it jerkily, skinned back, to a good twelve inches of fucking-flesh, dripping with the dews of desire.

With a simultaneous sigh of utter satisfaction from both youths, the peter was plunged once more deeply into the nest of nectary sweetness...this time all the way to the hairy root of the strong man's pleasure-piston! Ooooh, it felt so good!

They pumped together, groaning with the glory of the tingling sensation that thrilled belly and balls as their bodies slid in undulating union. Hercules felt the deep, warmth of the slimy sheath like a sucking mouth enveloping his peter in an omnivorous feast as he drove it in, and the draining drag of the anal tube as he withdrew lingeringly, and as the sweetness stung his balls he shivered with pleasure. And Equesto savored the plunging deliciousness of that dick, piercing deep into his bowels, seeming to send before it surges of dizzying feeling that made him cry out hoarsely with delight. The fucking belched between them with a ripeness of honey, and their loins melted into a oneness of utter exquisiteness.

The Centaur braced his front hoofs against the ground and rearing his body, his arms wound about Herky's neck and dragged his mouth down to merge with his whimpering lips in the rabid rapture of a thirsty kiss. And then as Hercules' arms fastened about Equesto, and Equesto's arms found their way about those broad shoulders, the two, still dredging kisses between murmurous lips, lay fully together pumping furiously, feeling the slimy suctioning sound of their parts, jazzing juicily in a pleasure that seemed to ooze up slowly from deep between their legs like the first hints of moisture of the hidden spring, dampening the soil. Then bubbling as the feeling festered eruptively near the surface as they began to cry out in senseless little squeals, and then bursting out like a fountain, spurting, shooting with a streaming sweetness as Hercules pissed his load.

With a sob he drove his dick as deeply into the massaging asshole as he could to plant his spermy seeds in his brother's belly, and as he felt the cream gushing out of his balls with the rich recurrence of thrills, he sobbed out deliriously, "I'm coming! I'm coming! Oh it feels so damned good!" Equesto was eating Herky's mouth with ravenous groans, not saying anything, but his brother felt the long, throbbing thickness of the stud-like cock thrusting out from between them, retchingly, and he heard the ripe splat of the horse-man's cum upon the ground.

For a long quivering moment they laid, glued deeply together, steeping in the snug, sucking gloving of their bodies, and Hercules felt the spinning, exhilarating thrill slowly draining out of his belly and limbs as his peter softened in the pocket of the Centaur's asshole. Their lips still touched in the wondering discovery of their first kiss, tasting the sweetness of mouths as their tongue explored the interiors eagerly, and their hands moved with loving lechery over the other's flesh. And between their bodies the strong young man felt the unrequited turgidity of Equesto's tool, for even though it had shot off in the excitement of Hercules' ecstasy, it was not truly relieved.

The muscular man reached down and fondled the pulsing prick, feeling its warm, hard-muscled stem, the taut, glistening burgeoning of the swollen glands bathed with its cummy slime, and the Centaur whinnied hysterically. His massive meat was tingling with eruptive electricity.

As Hercules severed the suturing swab of their lips and stood up over the horseman youth suddenly, Equesto asked nervously, "What are you fixing to do, Herky?" He could hardly believe there were any more thrills to possibly tingle his balls...but he had a few things to learn. As his brother lifted a muscled thigh and positioned his brown, succulent-looking asshole over the tip of Equesto's penis that stood up like the stallion's spear it was, the Centaur had a delight in store he had not even counted on, and he shivered with expectant ecstasy as glans and rectum touched, and his eyes almost ached in their sockets as he stared at the incredible sight of that enormous bulb of his peter driving deliciously up into the elastic spreading of the brown-ringed hole to suck it in!

Equesto could not restrain the soft scream of unutterable bliss as he felt his cock sinking into that tight, slimy-succulent cavity of his handsome brother's shithole. A thrusting torrent of thrills seemed to surge up through his own bowels with an enervating sweetness. He wound his arms more tightly about Hercules and dredged his quavering lips with a deep thirstiness into Herk's mouth, his tongue flashing about helplessly like a snake. Oh gods, his whole big body seemed to be slowly, deliciously drawn into the snug, swabbing sublimity of those practiced bowels!

But even the sophisticated strong man, with his surfeit of sex, was experiencing a deepness of delight he had not known was possible. He felt a shortness of breath, sobs of pleasure crowding in his throat, a suffusing of an excruciatingly sweet sensation through his belly and legs, as that huge dong drove deeper and deeper into his turds. He let his grip on Equesto loosen so that the weight of his body could impale his body more quickly on this thrilling lance of love.

Both youths moaned with a heavenly hysteria as they felt their parts sliding and touching far into the belly of the beautiful muscle-boy, and their mouths glued gluttonously in a frenzy of fucking-kisses....

Even if the throes of his threatening climax was jollying his testicles to juice, the Centaur felt it would be redundant to say he could no longer take it lying down, so with harsh, inarticulate whinnies he began to struggle to his feet, automatically pumping his glossy butt to keep his penis fucking in that delicious poop-pocket. And Hercules, having known the ecstatic energies of a fucker about to come...though let us hasten to say, never with a horse...quickly, expertly fastened his arms and legs about the Centaur's magnificent torso, and hung on for dear life!

True, this was apt to be a rather tiring position, but Equesto, rearing rapturously, and crying out with hysterical horse-sounds, was thrusting his ass back and forth like a mad machine, feeling his pounding peter sliding in and out of that marvelous man-hole, shooting thrills through his belly like waves overlapping themselves as they washed frettingly up on the beach. And Hercules, clinging tenaciously to the frantic creature, was able to get a few good licks in himself, driving that tool into himself so deeply and forcibly he gasped for breath and the pleasure rocketed through him with a delectable dizziness.

And then that massive, meaty penis surged swellingly, tightening in the asshole so much, each plunge was achieved only with terrific force, and the Centaur's load shot out with such ferocity and velocity it was all Herky could do to keep his senses about him. The thrill exploded in his brain with a brilliance of sensation that all but blinded him, and he screamed out as he felt his own prick jerking with a fierce convulsiveness as the tingling darts of feeling shot up through its shaft and the thick, creamy juice drained from its head in long ropes of milky liquid. And distantly about him, he heard Equesto squealing and babbling like an idiot of joy as his wad jetted deep in Herky's belly like a recurring geyser.

For a long time afterward, as they sank utterly drained of strength to the ground, the two brothers laid in weary contentment. A good sort of tiredness seeped through their quivering limbs, and between their legs a refreshing kind of exhaustion. Equesto's dick was still threaded deeply into Hercules' asshole, its limpness laved in the gentle contractions the strong man maintained lovingly for his partner's pleasure which was expressed through little catches of breath as the tube tightened and released about the long, meaty organ. And their hands caressed each other tenderly, Hercules stroking the sweat-wet glossiness of the horse-half of Equesto, while his lips kissed what might be termed the belly of his man-half, and Equesto's hand held and fondled the curly-haired head of his brother in what might be termed the truest of benedictions, so grateful he was for all that Hercules had done for him.

But finally with a sigh of sadness they slid apart since the Centaur's cock was slipping with a fat sluggishness from Herky's rectum, despite their closeness, and also the warm cum beginning to seep out was itching them a little.

For a moment they lay holding each other in loving arms, exchanging a frequency of tender kisses and gazing into the other's eyes with a fondness far more than brotherly. Hercules laid back grinning contentedly as he reached up and brushed back his brother's hair disarrayed by the ecstasies of love, as he felt Equesto's fingers exploring helplessly again between his legs. They trailed up and down the swollen stem, skinning the glans, curling about it as it began to resume a solidity of stiffness, and pumping.

"Now, we'll end this little idyll as we began it," the Centaur said softly, as he played affectionately with the throbbing thickness of the full erection. "You began by eating mine (he bent to kiss Hercules' moist, parted lips) so I'll end by eating yours!"

The muscular youth was limp with pleasant expectancy;

his eyes closed as he felt Equesto's fingers wrapping about his swollen penis and lifting it to the warm breath of his gaping lips. "Suck it, baby," he wept happily, "just suck it!"

No one had to tutor the horse-man in the art of blowing, Hercules decided with the first long liquid sucks of those lips down over and back up the eager nipple. For a bit he just lay there soaking into his body the goodness of that gobbling mouth that threatened to cut his tit right off at its hairy root. He moaned with exquisite agony as the lips slid upward, feasting furiously about the glans a moment, and then he sighed with satisfaction as the satin suction of the mouth fused down over the long tingle of the tail. His balls felt fluid like wax and his bowels like water, flowing to and fro with the submerging and emerging friction of that marvelous massage.

But then, like Equesto, he felt he had to get up on his feet or simply die of deliciousness, and so he stood up beside his brother, fully attuned to his thoughts, sank down on his front haunches and kept right on eating away. For the Centaur it was the very first dick he had ever sucked but he knew as he nursed it hungrily, feeling the hard, swollen contours of the marvelous penis with his moving lips, and tasting the seeping, salty juiciness of the head as he sucked it, this would not be his last!

And then Hercules felt it coming, rushing up irresistibly from the underside of his bag, a toppling sort of thrill that sapped the strength from his sturdy legs with its sweetness. So, with a gasping sob, he seized Equesto in his big hands and effortlessly rolled the cumbersome Centaur over on his back, and, quickly coming astride his chest, he plunged his penis back into the dripping gape of the thirsty mouth, and catching his brother's head in both hands he began working it back and forth in motion with the fucking thrusts of his own hips, sliding his tingling peter in and out between the munching lips. The eruptive ecstasy that electrified him between his spraddled thighs made him wild; he no longer thought about Equesto's comfort, but rammed his dick back and forth, back and forth in a frenzy as the end of his tool blew off. "Ooh shit, oooh shit," he squealed. "It's coming...

it feels so damned good...oooh shit, it feels so good!"

Equesto's mouth was so full of prick and creamy pee he couldn't say a word, but as he sucked and drank the testicle-honey ravenously, he couldn't have agreed more. And his dick surged up with a sudden fierceness of stiffness, jerking and the snowy semen shot up from the tip like bullets.

When it was over, and the surmounting sensations drained away mercifully, Hercules collapsed limply to his side. He was so utterly depleted and yet so utterly fulfilled he needed nothing so much, right then, but just to lie there, stupefied with sweetness, and rest for hours in the remembrance. He lay breathing deeply, his eyes closed. He had rolled away from Equesto and had really all but forgotten him. But then he heard a rustling sound, and a soft sigh of happiness.

He opened his eyes and then exclaimed with surprise, for the Centaur was gone, and in his place knelt a naked, utterly beautiful youth, smiling down at him. But he saw at once that it was still Equesto's handsome face, and glancing down between those golden, muscular thighs he saw the penis, reaching up erectly as vigorously, as heavenly huge as the Centaur's cock had been, and the gorgeous nuts dangled deeply, mule-sized as ever in their bag.

"Yes," the youth laughed, "I'm Equesto! I couldn't tell you before...but the last part of Hera's curse was that I would be released into my natural form only by the wholehearted, unselfish love of another human-being.... Herky, I'm yours, forever, if you want me!"

"Well, I'll be a horse's ass!" Hercules exclaimed joyously, his own dick leaping up aggressively in response to the apparent condition of his brother's cock. "Come here, baby," he sobbed, reaching for Equesto, "and you'll see how much I want you! Oh you doll! You doll! You living doll!"

As he rose to his knees, reaching, Equesto came quickly astride his thighs, and as their arms wound about each other like bands of steel, Hercules' penis drove deeply into the beautiful youth's asshole again and as they hugged, rocking together, fucking the tool into his belly, they wept for unfeigned, beautiful, fucking, sucking joy!

THE MORAL

The Moral of this little story is:

Don't ever be unkind to horse's asses...because some of them may not be horses' asses after all...but only Fairy Studs in disguise!

CHAPTER THREE
ESCAPE FROM REALITY

Escape from reality is the reason for almost every type pleasure. In the following story the writer combines the spirit of adventure with the phantasies of his own sexual imagination. Like most erotic pieces of this type, the improbability of the events is exactly what makes it exciting to the reader. It is interesting to note the minute detail the author resorts to in describing the rather impossible dimensions of the young hero, Tom. This type of fantasizing is very common in the erotic short story; it is usually the result of the writer's own subconscious desire to be the living image of his fictional hero.

The following is an adventure story which incorporates the romance of Tom and Mike. They are abducted by pirates and sold on the slave market in Tangiers. The reader will note that the author occasions several females to wander in and out of the story without purpose. Many psychiatrists conclude that the purpose for this is that it gives the writer justification of some sort for his unrestrained account of the homosexual experience.

ABDULLAH

The sun was just rising on the Mediterranean as young Tom Black came onto the deck of the sailing schooner, the Intrepid, recently sailed from Boston. Shipping as a cabin boy, Tom had already found the love of his life in the sea and this beautiful ship. A handsome blond boy of just seventeen years, Tom stood by the rail, stretched his well-muscled body, revealing the taut muscles of his body under the tight T-shirt and the hip-hugging pants which constituted his entire wardrobe. His eyes stretched toward the horizon and in the distance he saw another sailing ship. Calling out to the bridge he alerted the captain to the approaching ship.

Soon there was a crowd of sailors at the rail. Beside Tom stood his special friend, the dark, handsome, twenty-eight-year-old Black Irishman from Boston; Mike 0'Shea. Mike and Tom stood shoulder to shoulder and watched until a cry went up that the approaching vessel was a pirate ship. There was a scramble for cutlasses, just as the pirate ship came alongside; and when grappling irons were thrown and held the two vessels together, Mike put his arm on Tom's shoulder, turned Tom to face him, looked him directly in the eyes and said, "Mind you, be careful. I don't want anything to happen to you."

The battle lasted only a short time. Blackness enfolded Tom when a heavy wooden truncheon struck his head.

Consciousness returned slowly and Tom gradually became aware of the fearful stench of hot, sweaty, dirty bodies crowded in a small, evil-smelling room. He shook his head and tried to sit up, but gentle hands restrained him and in the dim light he could just make out the features of his friend, Mike. "Lie still, you'll be all right," said Mike.

"What happened?" Tom asked.

"We've been captured...all of those who are still alive. I think there are about twenty of us left. I don't know where we are going or what will happen to us...but we will stick together and things will work out some way," reassured Mike.

Tom lay back down and Mike lay beside him, cradling Tom's sore head on his muscular arm. Tom slept fitfully for the rest of the day, and by evening, when a meager meal was thrown to them, he was able to sit up and eat the food that Mike fed him. Soon he was sleepy again and lay back down, his naked body pressed tightly against Mike's hard, muscular body. They lay like this and soon were talking of home. Tom told Mike about his girl, the blonde and beautiful Nancy who was waiting there for his return. Mike asked Tom if he had ever slept with Nancy, and Tom said, "No," and Mike laughed and said, "You mean that you really are a virgin?" and Tom, embarrassed, agreed. Tom lay there on his back and was aware that the discussion had caused him to have an erection...and when Mike noticed it, he said, "Tom, you really have a piece of meat there. That's one of the biggest I have ever seen."

Tom replied, "When we were kids we used to play around a little and I always had the biggest one in our gang. We measured them once and mine is seven inches long when soft and grows to ten inches when it's hard."

Mike said, "I always thought mine was big, but you sure have me beat, see?"

Tom looked and saw that he wasn't the only one with a hard-on...Mike's cock was standing up hard and erect, too, and although it wasn't quite as long as Tom's, possibly an inch shorter, it was much bigger around.

One of the sailors sleeping nearby rolled over and said, "Shut up and let us get some sleep."

Mike and Tom lay back down and soon Tom was sound asleep again. He dreamed of Nancy, and in his dream he saw her coming across a field to him. He gently pulled her down on a pile of hay, slowly removed all her clothes, stripped himself, and then with the greatest of tenderness placed his cock against her waiting pussy and pressed in. The head had just gone in when he shot forth a great stream, flooding Nancy and gushing over both of them.

Tom awoke with a start and thought, "Now I'll be covered with the mess I always have on my chest and belly whenever I have one of those wet dreams." He reached down and found none of it on his body; his softening cock was slippery and wet, and he found that Mike was no longer laying beside him, but had turned the other way with his face near Tom's groin. Mike appeared to be sound asleep, but Tom wondered. He had heard about men doing things to each other, and many times on the voyage he had been approached by members of the crew, but he had always told himself that he was going to be true to Nancy. Could Mike have done this to him? The sensation had been the best he had ever experienced, and yet...and yet. He stretched and turned his body until he was pressed chest to chest with Mike, threw his arm over Mike's shoulders for warmth and drifted off to dreamless sleep.

In the morning, Mike awoke and looked at Tom, a tender smile playing over his handsome face. Tom awoke, looked at Mike and started to ask him the question, but before he could phrase it, they were all ordered up on deck. The twenty men, some with cuts and bruises, all stark naked, came out onto the deck of the ship. They were lined up and the pirate captain spoke to them; "You are all to be sold in the slave market here in Tangiers. I want you to clean up and I want you to look good. Any man who does not will receive ten lashes. There are buckets of salt water. Wash yourselves and then you will be given something to wear before you are taken to the market place."

The men did as they were told and when they had finished, they were carefully inspected from head to foot by the captain. He stood in front of Tom and said, "You should bring a good price. They like blond young things here, and with a prick the size of yours, someone is going to pay a pretty price for that hunk of meat." He ordered a sailor to bring a measure and had him record Tom's measurements: chest 44, waist 28, biceps 16, calves 15½, thighs 24, height 6' 1", weight 180. The captain gave instruction to measure the length of Tom's cock and it was 6½ inches. Then the captain told Tom he wanted the measurement when it was hard. Tom was so embarrassed that he was sure he couldn't get it hard. The captain reached for a whip and told Tom to get it hard. Tom took it in his hand and jacked himself off until his cock stood up hard and firm, and the sailor then measured it and said, "A good ten inches."

Then they moved to Mike who had the only really good body of the men assembled there. His chest was also 44, his waist was 31, his height 5'11"; his cock soft measured four inches, but grew to a full nine inches when Mike played with it under the captain's orders.

Each of the men was given a long piece of white cloth and told to wrap it around his waist. They did so and then were loaded into boats and taken to shore. They were chained together and led thru the city streets to the slave market place. Here they were thrown into a small cell where they were so crowded that they had to take turns sitting down. The cell had bars on all sides, and the people of the town came and stood outside and commented on each of the men and taunted them thru the bars.

Mike and Tom stood side by side, holding hands, reassuring themselves that so long as they remained together, everything would be all right. In the late afternoon they started taking the men one by one out of the cell, and the boys could hear the cries in the market place as the bidders purchased each man in turn. Finally, just Mike and Tom were left in the cell. Mike said, "Tom, remember this, I love you as only a man can love another man. I swear this to you, that somehow, in some way, I'll get free and come and find you and we will escape together." Mike was then led out and Tom stood alone and afraid. He heard the bidding going on and it took longer than it had for any of the other men. At last there was the cry of triumph, and Tom knew that his time had come.

He was led out of the cell, and when he asked the guard where Mike had gone, he was told that he had been bought by the local sultan and would undoubtedly be one of the sultan's guards. He said that Mike would be given good treatment if he did not break any of the rules, but that if he did, he would be tortured or killed.

Tom was led into the market place and onto a platform. There was a sea of faces around him, both men and women watching. There was a cry of delight from the audience when they saw this handsome blond...for they were all dark-skinned and a blond was a rarity much prized. The auctioneer read off all of Tom's measurements and commenting on his appearance said, "Here's something that should delight any woman or any man.

If the bidding goes over $500, then he shall be stripped for all to see." The bidding began and rapidly mounted. Tom stood there fearing that it would go up the figure mentioned, and as it neared that point, he felt himself turn red with embarrassment. When one man bid the $500, the auctioneer came over to Tom, unfastened the cloth around his waist, and throwing it to the ground, reached down with his dirty hand and held out Tom's cock for all to see. Tom felt as if he would die on the spot. There was a sigh of appreciation from the audience and bidding began again. After $750, there were just two bidders left. One was greasy, fat and repulsive, and the other a quiet little man who was buying slaves for the California mines. The bidding between the two went on until finally the fat, repulsive man bid $1000, and after a delay, the auctioneer announced that he was the buyer.

He came to the platform, handed over the coins, motioned Tom to put the cloth back on around his loins and to follow him.

Tom was revolted by the appearance of the man, but relieved at not being sent to the mines. He did not know what lay ahead, but he felt certain that it was better than being a slave in the mines, working fourteen hours a day, seven days a week, until one died.

He followed his master through the town until they came to a large walled-in area. The man unlocked the heavy door and led Tom into a compound. At the right was a long low building, and Tom was taken into a small room in this building, shoved into it, and locked in. There was no furniture except a small cot. Tom sat on the cot and felt nearly as if he would weep from the degradation he had experienced in the slave market when he had been forced to show himself nude before all the rabble, from the uncertainty of what lay ahead of him.

Finally he slept, and in his dreams he saw both Nancy and Mike; gradually Nancy faded from his vision and Mike, his hard-muscled dark body clothed in just a short tunic, his erect penis showing through the thin material, advanced toward him. Mike stepped just in front of him and raised the tunic, showing the magnificent cock standing out from his body, when Tom suddenly awoke at the sound of the door being opened. His own pecker was erect under the waistcoat he was wearing, and the man who had purchased him laughed at what he saw. He had a short tunic draped over his arm, like the one Mike had been wearing in the dream. He had Tom remove the loin cloth and put on a white tunic which was embroidered in gold. He gave Tom a pair of sandals to wear and motioned him to follow.

Following the man through the many corridors, he was finally ushered into a sumptuous room. At the far end, seated on a dais, was a handsome, prematurely gray-headed man, about forty years of age. He was sitting insolently on a large throne-like chair, dressed in a purple velvet robe, which was richly embroidered and covered with jewels. The robe was open to the waist and showed a heavily muscled chest and abdomen; held in at the waist and fastened below there, the robe fell open again exposing the man's firmly muscled legs. His only other garment was the thong sandals on his feet.

Tom was pushed forward and made to kneel at the feet of the handsome man. Tom realized that the man who purchased him was not his master, that it must be this rich and handsome man who owned him. He felt anger at having to kneel before any person, but yet was relieved to know that the fat, repulsive man was not his master.

The man on the dais spoke in English, "You are my slave. What is your name?"

"Tom Blake, of Boston," was the reply.

"Tom Blake, listen to me, and listen well. You are to do absolutely everything you are told. I will allow no objections of any kind. If you obey me, you will have comforts, fine food, riches, and beautiful clothes. If you disobey me, you will find death preferable to the tortures of my dungeon. Do you understand?"

Tom nodded and the man continued, "I am known as Abdullah the Magnificent. I maintain this household for the pleasure of myself and my friends. Since you are such a valuable commodity, you will be treated as a guest, but always, you must do my bidding."

Abdullah then clapped his hands and into the room came six huge black Nubians, dressed only in G-strings—narrow bands of ribbon around their waists and small pouches just covering their sex organs. They stood on either side of Abdullah, crossed their arms and looked at Tom. Tom had never seen such magnificent bodies as they had. Their muscles rippled beneath the black skin that was as shiny as satin. Their huge organs bulged in the small pouches containing them, the outline of each penis showing distinctly through the material.

Abdullah spoke to the fat, greasy, little man, "Bring Tom to me. I want to inspect him." The man grabbed Tom and pulled him forward until he stood directly in front of his master. "Remove his tunic," was the command.

Tom started to resist, then remembered the instructions he had just received. The tunic was unfastened at the shoulder and slipped to the floor. He stood there, his fair skin in striking contrast to the black skins of the slaves and the warm brown skin of his master.

Reaching forward, Abdullah took Tom's cock in his hand, ran his hands over Tom's balls, then up over his body. Then he turned Tom around and ran his hands over his back, over his buttocks, then probing with his finger, pressed it against Tom's asshole.

"Have you ever been fucked there?" he was asked, and Tom shook his head negatively. Tom was turned around again and Abdullah ran his hands up and down Tom's body, and fondled his penis some more. Tom felt a little tendency to harden his cock but it must have not been noticeable for Abdullah said, "He appears normal. I wonder how he will react to some female stimulation."

Abdullah again clapped his hands and into the room came a beautiful young maiden dressed in flowing scarves that revealed her lovely body and yet hid it from complete view. She came slowly across the room and knelt at the feet of Abdullah.

"This is my favorite slave girl, Meta. No one is allowed to touch her except at my orders. To do so without permission will mean death."

Abdullah motioned to two of the slaves and they sprang forward and pinioned Tom between them. Dragging him to a pillar in the center of the room, they put Tom's arm around the pillar and fastened his wrists through rings at the back. His feet were then fastened to rings in the floor. Except for his head, Tom couldn't move a muscle.

At a signal from Abdullah, Meta advanced slowly and sensuously toward Tom. When she reached him, she raised her hands and caressed his face, and then slowly and sensuously ran her hands down his body. The touch of her, even under the restraint of the chains, caused Tom's cock to rise, and in a minute it was standing at attention...its full length, hard and firm. Meta had not touched it, but she kept running her hands over Tom's hips, up his legs and through the pubic hair. The cock throbbed and finally Meta pressed it between her hands and slowly began to massage the head. Less than a minute elapsed before a great spurt of white cum shot out of it and struck her in the face and dripped down onto the silk garments she was wearing. She stood there holding the cock until it had completely quit shooting, and then sank to the floor at Tom's feet.

Abdullah then motioned her to leave the room, and getting up, came down to where Tom was fastened. "The next experiment will be to see how much you react to a man. Every man, under the proper circumstances, can be aroused by another man, and I intend to see you respond."

So saying, he motioned to one of the slaves to kneel at Tom's feet. The slave opened his mouth, and leaning forward, sucked Tom's soft cock between his lips. The warm mouth and the sucking motion and the novelty of it soon had Tom aroused again. He stood there as the slave continued to massage his hardening cock. It didn't take long until he felt himself almost ready to come. His body tensed, and as Tom felt himself shoot into the warm mouth, he noticed that Abdullah himself was aroused by what he was witnessing, and that Abdullah's own cock was showing hard under his robe, and as he moved to a different position, it came into plain view between folds of the robe. The slave sucked everything he could get out of Tom and then spit it out on the floor at Tom's feet, where there was already a puddle that had dripped off Meta and her clothing.

Abdullah said, "That was quite satisfactory. I think he will fit into our group very well, as he can be had either way." He then motioned to one of the slaves who went to the door and brought in three young dancing girls. These girls were naked, except for silken skirts which revealed more than they hid; their upper bodies and beautiful breasts were completely uncovered.

They began a dance, the very essence of which was sex. Closer and closer they danced, and then the three of them gathered around Tom and began to run their hands over his body. Six hands explored every inch of it. They began to suck on his cock, and it responded quickly to their treatment. Their hands played with his balls, fingers probed his ass, they kissed his nipples, the bottoms of his feet. Every square inch of his body. His cock was not completely hard, and they kept playing with it until it began to throb and for the third time shot its wad. This load was not as full as the last two had been, but it added several more spots to the floor in front of Tom's feet.

Abdullah commented, "He is doing very well. I want to find out just how many orgasms he is capable of during a day, and then we can judge just how much use he will be to us."

The experiment continued. This time it was a young boy, about fifteen years of age, who came over to Tom, played with his soft cock, sucked on it, and then jerked it until Tom finally gave out with his fourth load.

The fifth was induced by the three dancing girls again, using new techniques. Tom was so spent by this time that he was sure that he could not come again, but all of the Nubians went to work on him and continued until he had shot forth two more times, making his total seven. Tom then collapsed and, as he hung limply from his bonds, Abdullah realized that he had reached his maximum and he signaled to the slaves to remove the bonds, and when they did, Tom collapsed onto the floor. At a sign from

Abdullah, they carried him, still naked, on their hands above their heads. They moved out of the room and carried him into a bedchamber and laid him gently on the bed, face down. Tom lay exhausted, not caring as the slaves tied his hands and feet to the corners of the bed. Tom was left this way for only a minute before he heard the door open and saw Abdullah come into the room. Tom couldn't move, but he could hear the heavy robe fall to the floor and the bed sagged as Abdullah got upon it. Tom could feel him kneeling on the bed and then he felt something hard pressed against his ass. It could only be one thing. Abdullah had greased it up, and without too much effort, the head forced open the rim of the ass. Abdullah was gentle, but persistent, and Tom was so exhausted that he couldn't resist. The cock slid in farther and farther, and finally Tom felt Abdullah's full weight on him and could feel the huge, hard cock clear up inside him. Abdullah began to fuck and was gentle at first, but as the ass became lubricated, he became more and more violent until he gave a groan and plunged it all the way in, and Tom could feel it throb clear up inside him. Warm cream gushed out of the cock and bathed the burning rim of Tom's ass. Abdullah lay there for a long time, then slowly pulled out his cock and wiped it off. Releasing Tom, he pulled Tom close to him. Tom feel asleep in Abdullah's arms, and dreamed that he was being held by Mike.

In the morning when Tom awoke, he found himself still sleeping beside Abdullah. He felt a revulsion toward this man who had so foully abused him. He started to get up, as Abdullah, waking, said, "You may go. I shall send for you later in the day." Abdullah reached for a bell cord and in just a minute a slave appeared and Abdullah instructed him to show Tom his apartment.

For the next few days Tom saw Abdullah only occasionally, and during that time no demands were made on him. He was free to run around a certain part of the household, he had slaves to wait upon him, he could swim in the natural mineral pool. He was served sumptuous meals in his room. On the third day, as Tom was swimming in the pool, he was startled to see Meta enter the colonnade surrounding the pool. She stood there and watched Tom as he lazily swam in the water, his naked body showing in the sparkling water. Tom finally got out of the pool and went toward the girl. He started to get an erection as he came nearer to her, and could make out every curve of her body through the shimmering silk. Meta said, "You mustn't even talk to me...if we should get caught, it would mean terrible tortures for you. But I did want to see you and tell you that I think of you often." Tom had to resist the impulse to pull this beautiful girl to him, to smother her with kisses. Meta reached out and touched his hand and then turned and fled from his sight.

When Tom returned to his room he lay on the bed and all he could think of was Meta...and finding himself with a hard-on, he began running his hand up and down his cock, and before he knew what had happened, he had shot all over his body. He got up and cleaned himself and put on his tunic...the physical need gone but desire still there.

The following day was spent wandering around the area in which he was allowed. He hoped that he would at least catch sight of Meta, hoped he would be able to talk to her and arrange to meet her that night. It was to no avail, he did not see her all day.

In the early evening, Tom was lying on his couch when one of the black slaves came to his room and told him he was to have dinner with Abdullah. He was dressed in a fine, silken tunic which came just below his hips, but which was not long enough to cover him completely when he sat down. He was led to Abdullah's apartment where he was greeted cordially by his master. "This is the first opportunity I have had to really get to know you. Please make yourself comfortable."

Tom, whose guard was up and who faced this evening with a mixture of fear and eagerness, was thrown off guard by the manner in which he was met. He sat on a couch and Abdullah stretched out on another. A gourmet's dinner was served them and throughout the meal Abdullah kept up a pleasant conversation, asking about his home, his family, his interests. Gradually

Tom relaxed and enjoyed himself, the first time he had done so since leaving the ship.

Abdullah made no reference to anything sexual, even though, as they lay on their couches, their private parts were, from time to time visible to each other. Tom found himself watching Abdullah and looking at his body as revealed by the tunic, found himself thinking of Mike's similarly firm, hard, brown body, and to his chagrin, Tom found that he started to get a hard-on. It was not mentioned by Abdullah, but he could not have missed it.

Dinner over, Abdullah said that he thought it would be pleasant to have a massage and he called two of the slaves. They brought towels, perfumed ointments and creams, and astringents, and Abdullah, standing, pulled his tunic off over his head and lay down on the couch naked, and signaled to Tom to do likewise. The slaves were experts and they worked over every inch of the bodies with their hands. Abdullah's back was finished first, and when he rolled over onto it while the slave massaged his stomach, chest and groin, his cock began to rise and soon it stood up at full mast.

When Tom turned over, he saw what had happened and determined by force of will not to let it happen to him. However, the slaves hands went down on the inside of his legs, massaged the cream into his groin and then into his scrotum and at last his pecker was greased. This was too much. Tom could not help it but his huge prick got harder and harder and the slaves kept right on massaging it until it stood completely rigid.

Abdullah dismissed the slaves, and standing up, his own cock still hard, came over to Tom's couch, and knelt between Tom's legs and began to suck on the big cock that was standing up so firm and so ready. Abdullah then changed positions and lay with his head near Tom's feet, and after kissing Tom's cock, went all the way down on it, holding it firmly in this throat. Abdullah's own rigid shaft was right in front of Tom's face, but Tom kept his mouth firmly closed, determined that he would not touch it. Abdullah finally had Tom so close to coming that Tom was all set to shoot when Abdullah released his mouth from Tom's cock and said, "Now if you want to get your gun off, you are going to have to at least take mine in your mouth."

Tom was so hot, so ready and eager to come that he overcame his reluctance, and frantically reaching for Abdullah's cock, shoved the head of it between his lips. He found it wasn't repulsive after all...and just then Tom shot and pumped and pumped his hot load into the waiting throat. Abdullah sucked and sucked until there was nothing more to come out.

Tom let the cock drop out of his mouth as he lay back on the couch exhausted. Abdullah changed positions and pulled Tom into his arms. He lay there quietly for some time and slowly began to move his hands over Tom's body. There was no reaction for a while, but eventually Tom felt a stiffening in his cock and he also knew that Abdullah's shaft was harder than a brick as it pressed against his belly. Finally Tom's cock was up and ready for more. Abdullah again turned and this time Tom took Abdullah's stiffened cock at once and eagerly sucked its rosy head. More and more of it went into his mouth and he found it a wonderful sensation to have his own being sucked while having another large one being shoved down his throat. Tom felt himself start to come and at the same instant realized that a stream was shooting into his own mouth. As his own prick sent Abdullah a second load, the groin in front of him pressed forward, neatly shoving a cock clear down Tom's throat. He had no alternative but to swallow what was shot there and he found, to his pleasant surprise, that it was warm and sweet.

When Tom finally returned to his own quarters, he lay on his bed and couldn't sleep. Although he had come three times that evening, he found that as he lay on the bed he had a hard-on again. His thoughts kept returning to Mike—not to Abdullah whom he had just left. He kept wondering where Mike was, how he was, what he was doing. He longed to feel Mike's body, to hear his voice, to press his throbbing cock into some opening of Mike's body. He lay there and imagined himself standing nude as Mike walked across a long room toward him...Mike's handsome body clearly showing through a thin robe, Mike's hard cock protruding in front of him. As he imagined Mike getting closer and closer and then stopping directly in front of him and dropping his robe, Tom's fist closed over his cock, and aiming it straight up, shot a white-hot stream all over his chest and groin. Only then did he sleep.

A day later Abdullah sent for Tom and told him that he was having a party that night and that Tom was to take part in the exhibition. Tom was instructed to get plenty of rest during the day as he would get little during the coming night, and to report to the head slave right after he had had a light supper. Tom did as he was told and when he found the head slave, he found that he was not alone. All of the six big black Nubians were there, as well as Meta, and the young boy who had sucked on Tom when he was tied to the pillar when he had first entered the household, and five of the six young dancing girls.

The head slave had a list of instructions and he gave minute details to each one as to what his part in the performance would be. Tom was the second one to take part, and he was told that he was to give a swimming demonstration. He was led to a large gate, the gate was opened, and Tom saw a large swimming pool he had never seen before. It was lit with many torches, and at the far end he could see a large crowd of men and women, lying on couches, being served dinner by many nearly naked slaves. Tom did as he was instructed. He stood there until all eyes were fastened upon him, then slowly removed his tunic and stood in the light of the torches so that all could see his naked body. They stopped talking and watched as Tom dove into the pool and began to swim, first face downward and then on his back. He had been instructed that he was to keep swimming until his cock had gotten hard and when it did, he was to get out of the pool and come to the end where the guests were. He was then to stand there naked, cock erect, and wait for further instructions. Tom played with his cock when he was underwater and it was soon hard and rigid. He swam to the end and slowly pulled himself out of the water and stood at the side of the pool, his magnificent cock sticking straight out in front of him.

Abdullah motioned him to come to him and when Tom did, Abdullah leaned up from the couch where he was lying with a nearly naked girl, and taking Tom's cock, pressed the head of it into his mouth and lovingly caressed the head. He then told the crowd that he was going to have Tom go around the room and anyone who wished to could play with or suck the cock for half a minute. If anyone was able to bring Tom off, then Tom would be given to that person for the evening when the entertainment was over. He told Tom to start around the room, and Tom did so, going from one couch to another. Some of the women tried to jack him off, some even licked or sucked his cock. The men nearly all sucked on it, but each time they would just about get it throbbing and ready to come, the half minute would be over, and as Tom moved to the next couch, the brief respite would prevent him from coming. Tom had nearly circled the room and was trying to prevent his coming, even though he found both the men and women's attention very exciting. When he reached the last man in the room, he was just about to ready to shoot when Abdullah called time again. Tom turned to Abdullah for instructions and the girl who was lying beside Abdullah said, "I haven't had my turn." Abdullah glowered, but said to Tom, "Go ahead." The sight of her lovely body, covered only with the sheerest silk, got him uncontrollably hot, and when this girl pressed all of the cock she could into her mouth, Tom let go and there was no doubt that she had made him come as Tom gave her such a load that it ran out the corners of her mouth and down her chin.

Tom, looking triumphantly at Abdullah, was satisfied, but he also felt a shudder of fear go over him as he realized that this man would not soon forgive or forget that Tom had attracted the young, beautiful woman, when Abdullah had obviously intended to use her for his own later gratification...and that by the terms of the game, she could have Tom all night if she wished.

Tom then retired from the area and returned to the head slave.

He assumed that he would have nothing to do until the festivities were over, but he found that such was not the case. He was told to lie down and rest and that he would be a participant in the finale of the evening. Meanwhile, the young boy had gone out with Meta, and Tom had heard the instructions given to them, that Meta was to lie in the shallow part of the pool while the boy fucked her...literally a water-cooled fuck. Other items followed on the program...singles and doubles being sent out to perform what was required of them. Two of the dancing girls were sent out absolutely naked and made to lick each other's pussies until they each had orgasm.

Finally everyone had participated at least once and all had returned. Tom wondered what lay in store for him with the sexy woman who had claimed him for the whole night with her. His reveries were interrupted when he and the others were told that the finale was ready to begin. Each of the six—Tom, three slave girls, the young boy who Tom found was named José, and another young man who appeared to be Spanish or Italian—all were dressed in tunics, over which were placed heavy velvet robes. They were led out into the dining area and made to stand in a line with their backs to the pool, facing the guests.

Abdullah then pinned a number from one to six on each of them, and Tom was number six. Then the guests were each given a slip of paper, but most of them were blank except for six which had numbers on them. Now the six big Nubians came into the rear and stood in front of each of the six who had first appeared. Abdullah then informed the guests who drew a number could direct the Nubians to do anything they wished with the person in front of them.

The Nubians were dressed in their usual costume...the brief, fully packed G-string, each had been sex-starved for days. The man who had No. 1 got up and walked over to the Nubian standing in front of No. 1, one of the dancing girls. He whispered into the slave's ear, giving his instructions. The slave bowed low, then reached down and tore the G-string from his waist, allowing his magnificent black pecker to flop into full view. He then advanced to the girl, picked her up, carried her to a couch, and slowly removed every stitch of her clothing. His cock having reached its full dimensions by then, he knelt over her, his cock aimed at her face, but then he lowered his hips, guiding his prick into her and began to fuck. She moaned, despite her efforts not to show the pain she was in...the size of that cock must have made her feel as if she were being plugged with a forearm. The Negro fucked and fucked and finally shot forth his stream, which filled the gap and ran down between her legs. As soon as he had quit shooting, he pulled out his cock and shook it all over the girl. They both got up from the couch and went back and stood beside the pool, absolutely naked, white cum dripping down her legs, his cock still glistening from the cream of it.

Number 2 was called immediately and this time it was one of the female guests who had the number. She called the number 2 slave over and spoke to him, and he went back to the victim which was the darker fellow Tom hadn't seen before. The slave removed all of the Latin's clothing, and then kneeling down, began sucking on a cock no larger than a little finger which swelled in size until it was eight inches long and an incredible three inches thick. The slave took the whole thing into his mouth and hungrily devoured the cock until everyone could see the Latin shaking with an impending orgasm and then give an ecstatic moan as he shot his wad into the throat which surrounded his cock. All this time the slave had kept on his G-string, but when the Latin came, the slave got so excited that his cock burst the strings and a tremendous 11½" of prick stood up black and ready, but there was nothing to do with it.

Number 3 was called and one of the Nubians was instructed to kneel in front of the slave girl who wore that number. She had to suck him off, but his cock was so large that she couldn't do more than put the head in her mouth and use her hands to jack him off. But it was effective, and he shot almost immediately snow-white cum streaming out of the corners of her mouth and down her chin.

Number 4 had the young boy, José, and the Nubian do a 69, lying on the marble patio beside the pool. The black body of the Nubian and the lighter body of the boy were beautifully silhouetted against the white marble. They lay on their sides, their cocks in each other's mouths. Then José got on top and drove his cock into the Nubian's throat while he went down as far as he could on the black shaft he had shoved between his lips. Their orgasms were simultaneous and the black man must have shot a huge load, for it dripped out of José's mouth as he collapsed on the black body, his cock all the way down in that throat.

Number 5 was next and the slave followed his instructions and stripped the last of the slave girls. Then he stripped himself and stood facing her, his cock growing to huge dimensions. Then, pulling her to an archway, he fastened metal bands around her ankles and wrists. He pulled her arms up over her head and fastened her hands to hooks in the arch; her legs were spread wide and secured to rings in the floor. She hung there, unable to move as the black man advanced toward her, his cock standing out a good 12 inches, hard, glistening, a drop of white on the head of it where he had oozed just from the excitement of getting things ready. He pressed against her front, guiding his pole into her waiting slit. As he pressed inch after inch of it into her, her hips pressed backward and she let out a scream of pain at the stretching of her arms. The slave showed no mercy... he forced his entire cock inside her until his hard, black body pressed tightly against her, every inch of him inside her. He reached around behind her and grasping her naked buttocks, pulled them toward him every time he fed her a foot of cock with every stroke. He kept this up for a long, long time, and when he had finally reached his climax, she had had nearly seven orgasms, and when at last he pumped it to her, before slowly withdrawing his cock, she slumped into a faint as he walked away from her and left her hanging there by the arms.

By this time the guests were all aroused and many of them were pulling up their clothes and fondling each other. An orgy was in the making and there remained only one exhibition before they would start their own.

The man who had number 6 called the last Nubian to him and Tom watched as the slave was given his instructions. The man who was giving the instructions crossed over to Abdullah, whispered to him, and Abdullah nodded in the affirmative. He gave instructions to the slave who left the room and came back with a long black table which was placed in front of the guests. The slave then walked over to Tom and slowly pulled his tunic up and over his head and stripped him, for all to feast their eyes on. He then grabbed Tom and lifted him in his arms and carried him to the table and lay him face down on it. Tom found, to his surprise, that there was a hole cut into the center of the table, and his cock and balls, which although aroused, were not completely hard, fit through, and hung down below the table. Tom's arms and feet were tied onto each corner of the table. Then a wooden block with a recessed section in the center was placed under Tom's chin, so that his head was forced back off the table.

Tom lay like this, fearing that whatever was to be done to him would involve being fucked in the ass...and he sweat from fear as he had only been fucked the one time by Abdullah when he was so completely worn out that he had been unable to do anything but relax and let Abdullah have his pleasure.

Now the slave who was arranging all this called the number 2 slave who had blown the Latin but not gotten off his own nuts. He also called over slave number 1 who had fucked the first girl. This slave walked to the head of the table and taking his limber cock, forced it into Tom's mouth. Tom thought to himself, "This isn't going to be too bad, I guess I'm getting off luckier than I thought, but why all this table bit?"

He was soon to find out. The slave in charge got up on the table and knelt above Tom. In his hand he held a jar of grease which he liberally applied on the most glorious thirteen inches of cock God ever created, and he also liberally applied the grease to Tom's ass. The slave who had had his cock in Tom's mouth got under the table, and lying on his back, could reach up and draw Tom's cock into his mouth. Slave number 2 moved into position at the head of the table, and shoved his hard, unrelieved cock so far into Tom's mouth that Tom gagged. He didn't know how to handle that much cock, but just then, he felt his asshole being spread, and knew that the slave above him was going to do just one thing.

All other things were forgotten, even his own cock being sucked below softened, even under the stimulation, and he forgot about the luscious pecker in his mouth. All he could feel was the size of the pecker being forced inside him.

Inch after inch went inside him...six inches, ten inches, twelve inches, and not being able to stand it anymore, Tom screamed from the pain. The slave withdrew half of it, but still kept the head in there. The pressure and the suction on Tom's cock continued and it began to respond and Tom really sucked on the cock in his mouth. When the slave on top began pressing again, nearly all of his shaft went in before Tom screamed again. This time the slave did not pull out but left all of about eleven inches in Tom and held it at that point. Tom relaxed a little and with a savage lunge the whole thirteen inches went into him with the Nubian's balls slapping the sides of his legs and feeling like they must be the size of a bull's. He felt as if he had been split in two and that he had pecker coming out of his ears.

Now movement began, and Tom could feel that thing so far up inside him that he wondered if he were human. As the strokes became longer, Tom heard a sigh of appreciation from the audience as they watched nine, eleven, and even thirteen inches of black cock come out of his white asshole and then plunge all the way in, out of sight.

Tom found that his own cock, massaged from without and from within was harder than he had ever known it to be...it was throbbing, and he felt that he could shoot at any minute and yet he found that he didn't want this to end. He wanted to feel that big black cock shoot in him, he wanted to let go of his own load, and yet he wanted this fantastic joy ride to go on forever. Finally Tom felt a load of hot cum shoot into his mouth and he became aware of the warm pungent cream being deposited there and as he gulped, 11½" of thick, hot cock went sliding down his throat. He could feel the cock pump, expanding and contracting as more shot out. And just then the magnificent pecker up his ass exploded and there was a frantic pulsing going on in there as more was poured into him at that opening. Such a load of cream going into him meant that something had to come out and his own cock shot...he felt a stream of twelve ecstatic bursts gush from clear up inside him, gushing into the thirsty throat of the Negro below the table.

No one even tried to make a move...they lay there like that for a long time until all the throbbing and pumping had ceased. Then the slave pulled away from the head of the table, and the slave beneath the table got up, and the one on top pulled his pecker out of Tom's ass, while white cum and red blood flowed out of it between his legs. Tom was completely exhausted; he couldn't have moved even if he tried.

Now the party broke into an orgy. Each of the guests who had won one of the slaves came to claim his reward. The girl got up from Abdullah's couch and came over to where Tom still lay tied. She pulled off all her garments and crawling under the table, sucked on Tom's limp prick, trying to get any cum that was left. Then climbing onto the table, she licked Tom's ass, her warm tongue soothing the violated rim. Getting off the table, she stood in front of Tom, pressing her pussy, hot and flaming, before Tom's face. Tom tried to avoid it, but she was the master, so Tom stuck out his tongue and began to slip it in and out of her hot crack.

She had Tom untied and led him away to a bed chamber. There she lay down on her back seductively and Tom advanced toward her, his cock rising with every step. There was no need to order him to do anything. What she wanted he was ready to give her. His cock rammed into her and she gave a moan of pain and satisfaction. Tom, having come several times during the evening already, didn't shoot his wad right away, but kept fucking for all he was worth, and every time he would drive down especially hard, she would cry with joy as he jammed it in up to the hilt; she had orgasm after orgasm, but Tom kept right on ramming it to her. Finally, things started happening in his loins, and when his cock swelled larger than it had ever before, the girl started screaming as she felt the flood begin. The hot sticky cream poured into her, bathing her inflamed sheath. Her twat was so full of cock that the fluid washed out of it and ran between her legs. Tom collapsed on her, breathing heavily. Finally, Tom rolled away from her onto his back, completely exhausted, and they slept like this for the rest of the night.

There was no special activity in the household on the next day. Everyone seemed to have had all the sex they could handle. Tom was exhausted, and yet he found that as he wandered around with little or no clothing on, he kept getting a hard-on, thinking of all he had seen and participated in the night before.

That afternoon he went for a swim in the pool, naked as usual. While he was in the pool, the young boy, José, came to the edge of the pool, slipped off his tunic and dove in. The boys compared notes as to what had happened the night before and José said that he had ended up in an orgy with one of the lady guests and one of the Nubian Slaves. The lady had ordered José to fuck her, to loosen her up and then she had the Nubian climb on her and he had rammed his huge cock into her and fucked her three times without stopping. Then she had ordered the Nubian to fuck José, which he did and José said he was still sore even though the slave didn't have a real hard-on. He said if he had, he wouldn't be able to walk. While the Nubian was fucking José, the woman let him shoot into her mouth. Then the woman made the slave pull out of José and stick his still hard cock into her again. She had gone to sleep that night with the Nubian's cock in her pussy and José's in her mouth.

José told Tom that Meta was terribly hot to go to bed with him and that if he would come to José's room that night, he would try to sneak Meta in.

While they were talking, they had stood in the shallow end of the pool and both of them had hard-ons. José ducked under the water and Tom felt him press his mouth over his rigid prick which was just below the surface of the water. José kept sucking, coming up for air when he had to, then down he would go again. Tom stood there, afraid of being seen, but thrilled at the treatment he was getting. Finally, he was ready to shoot, and he did so right into José's mouth. José came up right away, coughing and gasping for breath, white cum running from his mouth.

* * * * * * *

For the rest of the day, Tom kept playing with himself, thinking of having that beautiful girl, Meta, to satisfy him.

He went to bed, and then when everything was quiet, he sneaked down the hall to José's room. When he entered it, he saw Meta lying on the bed, naked, her arms held up to Tom... Tom stripped in an instant, threw himself into the bed and pulled Meta into his arms. They turned on their sides and Meta threw her legs over Tom's body. Tom's cock, hard and ready, slipped into her without any preliminaries. They lay like this for a long time, the head of his prick just inside her slit while they gently rotated their bodies, kissing passionately, Tom's hands fondling her breasts. The stimulation was too much. Tom shot. When he did, he rolled her on her back and buried his prick inside her the full distance.

Just as Tom's prick quit pumping, José stepped out from behind a curtain and said, "That was wonderful. I wish you could have another go, but this is too dangerous. Tom, you must go back to your room at once before you are discovered."

"What about Meta?" Tom asked.

"Oh, it's all right for her to be here," José explained, "She's my sister."

* * * * * * *

About two weeks later Tom was called in to see Abdullah. There was just one other guest at dinner, a distinguished-looking man who sat on a dais opposite the one on which Tom's master sat. Standing behind Abdullah were four of the Nubians, dressed in the usual white G-strings. Standing behind the other guest were four fair-skinned guards, their chests bare, dressed in very short red skirts. Tom looked and was startled. One of the guards was Mike! Their eyes met, but Mike gave his head an almost imperceptible nod, and Tom realized that they were both in danger if they betrayed their knowledge of each other.

Tom had been brought in for the amusement of the guest. Abdullah directed that Tom be stripped and tied to the pillar, as he had been forced to do the first time he was presented to the master. Mike's eyes never wavered from Tom's face. Tom was forced to stand there while two Nubians sucked him off. Then he was bound with his face to the pillar while the two others fucked him in the ass. Tom had had to take a cock there so many times that he found he could do so without too much strain, but he hated to have Mike see him in this position.

When the four of them had finished with Tom, he was led away, still naked. He returned to his room and lay on the couch and thought about Mike, and found that his prick was hard again. He grasped it and played with it while he had visions of what it would be to feel Mike's body against his own, knowing now what he didn't know when he had been aboard ship. He shot all over himself and let it dry there, imagining that it was Mike's cum that had covered his chest.

* * * * * * *

The next day Tom was passing down the hall to the pool when a slave slipped him a piece of paper into his hand. It was a message from Mike. "I have made arrangements for our escape. Trust this slave. Do as he says and be ready at midnight tonight."

Tom looked at the slave who nodded his head, and returned to the apartment without taking a swim. He was in a fever of excitement. How would Mike make arrangements; where would they go; would they be able to make it; what lay ahead for them?

Tom knew that if they could just get together, life would have meaning again. The hours crept by slowly. Luckily, Tom wasn't called for sexual duty that evening, so he retired at about ten, lying quietly on the couch without sleeping. Finally midnight arrived and Tom heard a rustling in the room. He couldn't see the black slave but felt a hand on his shoulder, which also lovingly explored his crotch. A voice whispered into his ear that he must put on a black cloak, and Tom put on the one held out to him. It had a hood, which Tom pulled as far over his face as he could. He followed the slave down the hall, through the narrow passages until they came to a side gate which the slave opened. Tom stepped out and met another black clad figure. Mike held out his arms, and Tom slipped into them. Their faces met for an instant, and then Tom felt Mike pull him along the street. They moved quickly, but did not run so that they would not attract attention. Eventually they made their way to the shore, where there was a small boat guarded by two men. Mike and Tom got aboard and Mike threw a bag of money to the guards as they cast off. They put up the black sail and headed for sea.

Mike said, "We have provisions, water and food for six days. We can sail for Italy or one of the islands between here and there." They set the sail, lashed the tiller, and Mike said, "Now."

He held out his arms again and Tom moved into them without hesitation. Their bodies pressed together. The clothes they were wearing did not insulate the warmth that passed between them. Mike's mouth closed over Tom's and his tongue entered Tom's mouth. Tom ground his body even more tightly against Mike's, and he felt his own pecker so hard and firm between them, pressed against something equally hard and hot attached to Mike. Their hands started moving over each other's body. Mike reached down and ran his hand up Tom's legs, lifting the tunic he was wearing under his robe. He pushed the robe off Tom's shoulders, and then his other hand continued upward until Tom felt Mike grasp his balls before lovingly taking his throbbing pecker in his hand. Tom's own hand repeated the operation, except that he found Mike wasn't wearing anything.

CHAPTER FOUR
PETE

Pete falls somewhat short as an erotic story, and not only in length. While it managed in its all too brief course to bring in the standard variations—active and passive roles in fellatio, active and passive roles in anal intercourse—it does not employ the sort of detail typical of these stories.

Even more unusual is the deliberately literary style used by the author. This anonymous creator can write, and does so for the most part. He employs a romanticism not customary in this field. The first two pages of a six page story are sans sex. They describe a romantic friendship that develops over a long period of time; most such stories involved an initial meeting which progresses almost at once to sexual activity.

But for all these lackings, Pete earns its place as a Tijuana Bible story through the same means as every other story in this collection—its ability to arouse, and its insight into the human—and especially homosexual—sexual psyche.

* * * * * * *

There are some guys you meet, have once—and never forget. And there are others you spend a lot of time with doing a lot of things—and you can't even remember their names. I guess you never forget the first ones—your first blow job, your first taste of cock, the first time you got your dick into a warm and willing asshole, the first time you had your own cheeks spread by a hot piece of meat....

I remember all those "firsts" damn well, and a few of the other "specials" too. Then there are the ones whose names are forgotten—but not what they did! I remember the young Air Force boy who looked so innocent and lonely at the bar, who was lonely enough to go home with me, who was drunk enough to let me take down his pants and drain the virgin load from his beautiful cock, who fell asleep in my arms afterward. I remember the sailor who stripped down as soon as we got home and wouldn't let me do anything but fuck him all night long. I remember the butch policeman who slept with my dick in his mouth and sucked it down every time it got hard. I remember the tough youngster with the motorcycle uniform who came all over the shower and then begged me to use his juice instead of Vaseline. I remember the rugged young marine with the body of a Greek god and a knob on the end of his cock like an egg, who got hottest when I played rough with his balls, who made love like a tiger, who fucked me again and again, and each time was better than the last.

I remember cheap hotel rooms with squeaking beds, tiled-walled YMCA showers, luxurious apartments with carpets like mattresses, blankets hastily spread out under the stars, the sun-drenched deck of a swimming pool...and so many other places.

But most of all, I remember a stormy night, and Pete.

The first time I met Pete was at an informal party that started one Saturday at brunch and went on and on until it was dawn of the next day. I remember finding him alone in a corner, looking for all the world like an out-of-place farm boy in loose-fitting sweat-shirt and khaki trousers. He was in his early twenties with sparkling blue-gray eyes, a wide, easy smile and features that were ruggedly masculine. He had short clipped, sandy hair and a well-tanned complexion, and I soon found myself talking with him as if I'd known him for years. I can remember wondering afterward why I didn't put the make on him right away. As it was, I went out to refill a drink, and when I came back, Pete was gone. I asked one of the guys what had happened to him.

"Did you see that beautiful sailor who walked in? Well, your friend Pete looked him over for a minute, walked over and said about ten words to him—and they left together. Yeah, some shy farm boy!"

I began running into Pete at parties and various bars after that, and we got to be good friends. Then we started going places together—movies and dinners and things like that—and several times I ended up spending the night on his couch with some trick while he worked out with another one in his bedroom. Maybe I thought I'd gotten to know Pete too well to have sex with him, but more than once I found it was more fun just to sit and talk with him than to land some attractive sack-stuff.

One night Pete and I set out to do the town and ended up closing one of the bars. We headed for his place for a night-cap, and his car ran out of gas a couple of blocks away. It was raining like hell, and we were both drowned by the time we got to his little house. He put me to work in the kitchen mixing a couple of strong drinks, and when I came into the living room, he had a good fire going in the fireplace. He brought a couple of large bath towels, and we began stripping off our wet clothes and drying off. Suddenly I was aware that this was the first time I'd ever seen Pete even partially naked.

Pete's shoulders were wide and thickly ridged with muscle and his arms were powerfully developed. His chest was broad and full, and a light covering of sun-bleached hair spread between the large, flat nipples at either side. His stomach fell away flat and taut from the heavy curves of his chest, and his torso tapered neatly to his hips. I was keenly aware of the rugged masculinity of his body, and I wondered if he sensed the tension mounting within me. He dropped his trousers, and his white boxer shorts shone in sharp contrast to his bronzed flesh. I swallowed deeply from my drink and tried to concentrate on stripping and drying off.

"How about a little music?"

I looked up and saw him in front of the phonograph, his back toward me, completely naked. His smooth, sleek flesh was taut over his muscular back and turned from a deep tan to a soft olive color over his trim-curved ass. He started a stack of records and then turned, rubbing his towel over his head and face and laughing happily.

The soft trail of hair over Pete's belly broadened at his groin into a wide patch of crisp, dark, pubic hair, and his cock hung down from among it, thick and firm and loose, falling free and relaxed, its powerful length topped with a broad, full head. His balls were large and swung loosely between his solid thighs. I felt nervous and trembling inside, and I forced myself not to stare as I roughed the towel over my nakedness.

I crossed to the fireplace and stood there letting its warmth sweep over me. Then I felt Pete's hand on my shoulder, and as I turned, he was gazing deep into my eyes, a gentle smile on his lips. His arms slipped around me, pulling me to him, and his mouth found mine.

We stretched out on the floor before the fireplace, the room dark except for the reflection of the dancing flames on the walls and ceiling, the stillness broken only by the soft music from the phonograph. We lay there and sipped our drinks and talked, and from time to time, our bare flesh met, our lips, our mouths, our tongues.

I remember lying back as Pete bent over me, running his fingertips over my face, my neck, my shoulders, my body. I remember the pleasure of his touch, the warmth of his lips, the damp firmness of his tongue. I remember the ease with which his mouth found my cock and nursed it to rigid potency. I remember the pulsating excitement as he ran his tongue along the insides of my thighs and kissed my throbbing nuts. I remember the trembling sensations as he lay back and let me inspect his nakedness, as I touched the warm, smooth flesh, as I found the mysteries of his body, as I brought his massive cock to passionate hardness. Then I was lying on top of him, my arms and legs about him and his about me, and I felt him grip my dick and place it upright beside his, and they were equally large and solid and potent. Then we were lost in the fury of being together, nakedness to nakedness, desire matched by desire. And the precious liquid came pouring from within us at the same moment.

Pete lay on top of me, his flesh warm and damp with sweat against mine, and his hands wandered over my nakedness gently. I felt a wonderful satisfaction fill me as my breathing slowed again and my heart stopped its mad pounding. At last Pete sat up with a sigh, and I watched him pick up one of our towels and wipe his body lazily. Then he bent over me and carefully dried the huge pool of thick liquid covering my belly and dripping down into my crotch. "Between the two of us, we must have unloaded about a cup of juice!" he exclaimed, and then he began fingering my relaxed genitals. "Now I know why your friends call you Stud!"

"You're no midget yourself!" I chuckled. "Hell, I guess we're just about even."

"Yeah, and I'm glad we are!"

He bent forward and kissed the head of my dick lightly and then stretched out beside me once more. We embraced and talked quietly, contentedly, and at length we drifted off to sleep.

It was still dark and rainy when I woke, and the embers in the fireplace were sputtering and dying. I rose on one elbow and gazed down at Pete still sleeping peacefully beside me. I felt warm and comfortable watching his powerful chest rise and fall gently with his soft breathing, the handsome features of his face, the rugged muscle-hard lines of his body, the magnificent maturity of his genitals. It was as though I were enjoying a special secret, a unique pleasure. I touched him lightly, running my fingers over the silky chest hair, the smooth, sleek flesh, the relaxed fullness of his cock and tempting firmness of his balls. I wanted the thrill of having him!

I twisted about opposite him and pressed my lips to the sturdy head of his dick and let my tongue wash over its smoothness. He sighed and moved slightly in his sleep. I opened my mouth and drew in the soft length of his organ, sucking on it gently and feeling it slowly stretch and grow firm. He woke with a start, and then his cock was huge and throbbing with inner strength, filling my mouth and pressing into my throat. I sucked on it wildly, wanting to drink its precious cream like a man crazed by thirst. Gasping with excitement, he sat up and bent forward, gripping my head to keep my lips around the base of his pulsating rod. His body trembled and I could hear his heavy breathing clearly, and then he threw himself on me, wrapping his arms about my hips and taking my rigid cock into his mouth eagerly. The combination of sensations was maddening as each of us urged the other on to furious climax.

Suddenly I knew the ultimate moment had come! Pete's hammer jerked in my throat as if it were about to explode, and I could feel the aching desire in my groin take solid form and come driving to its summit. I wanted to scream, to merge my body with Pete's, to swallow his organ completely and have him drain mine totally. Then, at the same moment, twin eruptions burst from within us...geysers of virile liquid...wild explosions of hot cream...again and again...a potent flood filling my throat while his lips and tongue drew out every possible measure of mine...fireworks of passion searing the darkness which wrapped about us...ecstasy...and madness!

Pete and I had made a date to play cards at his place the next night with some friends, and they were already there when I arrived. We drank and talked and played, and all I could think about was how much I wanted to have Pete's body again. At last they left, and after a final nightcap, Pete and I turned out the lights and went into the bedroom.

Pete stood before me in the darkness, legs wide-spread, a broad grin on his face, and I undressed him, unbuttoning his shirt and running my hands over his magnificent torso, dropping his trousers and touching the muscular hardness of his thighs, pulling down his shorts and playing with the huge, relaxed organs hanging loosely from his groin. Then he began to strip me, and I held his cock and felt the excitement grow within it until it was stiff and dripping with power.

We were alone and naked, and all the desire we had had to

hold back came bursting forth as we fell on the bed. We thrashed about wildly, seeking to find the greatest passion, to give the greatest pleasure. For what seemed like hours, our delight seemed to have no bounds and no climax.

Then Pete was on his knees between my legs, his lips caressing my throbbing genitals, and suddenly he reared back, every muscle of his handsome physique taut with excitement.

"I've gotta have you all the way, Stud!" he gasped. "I want you completely."

My gaze fell to the huge, thick organ rising rigidly from his groin, the hard, rounded knob on the end of it almost bursting with tenseness. "Yes, Pete, yes!"

I closed my eyes as he got up from the bed, and in an instant my mind reeled to other times. Being held down while Art spread my cheeks for the first time. Those painful experiences as I became accustomed to the act. The ache filling me as Ben forced my legs high in the air and tried to jam his powerful organ into my unyielding hole. The men who had screamed as I had used them—and Pete's cock was as big as mine....

Then Pete was on the bed with me again, taking me in his arms, caressing me repeatedly, making love to me beautifully. He lay on top of me and his mouth covered mine and his tongue thrust against mine, and then I was aware of his lubricant-covered finger pressing between the cheeks of my ass and against the firm lips of my hole. And the lips parted. He reamed me gently but thoroughly, and all the time my only thought was of pleasing him and finding my own pleasure in the knowledge of his.

I remember little more. He knelt between my legs and lifted me back on my shoulders. He guided his cock between my cheeks and there was a moment of stabbing pain as the head of the instrument found the tight hole. Then with remarkable ease, it slipped in. Our bodies were one.

It took a wonderfully long time, but when Pete finally came, it was complete and perfect in every way. And later during that same night, I woke up to find him carefully coating my rigid cock with Vaseline; he had only tried taking it twice before, but I couldn't remember a greater pleasure than having my come pour into his body and feeling his spew out against my belly.

A week later I moved in with Pete; and no matter which way he turns, he's still the greatest!

CHAPTER FIVE
LEARNING THE HARD WAY

Learning the Hard Way repeats several of the themes common to such material-introduction to sex (or specifically to homosexual sex) complete with lack of reservations or guilt, and even a forcible introduction to anal intercourse which, despite the force and the pain, proves quickly to be pleasurable.

The use of such force, particularly where anal intercourse is concerned, is quite common in these stories. Most such erotica touches upon sadism to some degree, and the implication is that the homosexual personality by its nature contains a sadistic element that reveals itself in these fantasies.

Uniforms too are common—football, policeman, serviceman, fireman—the man in uniform seems to represent an excessive masculinity. Likewise all of the characters in these tales are highly romanticized, utterly masculine, hard-muscled, generously endowed. In the same light, a heterosexual author preparing such tales would describe females with large breasts, voluptuous hips, long soft hair—in short, the attributes of exaggerated femininity.

* * * * * * *

When I was still a kid in high school, I was pretty well built and hung, and it didn't take me long to find out what that hot equipment between my legs was for. My first lesson was from one of the other guys on the football team. We were horsing around in the gym one afternoon after everyone else had left, and when I grabbed for his crotch, he went right after mine. Then suddenly he straightened up and let me get a good feel, and the next thing I knew, he was unzipping my pants and sticking his hand right inside my shorts. I'd never had a guy grab me bare before, but it felt awfully good, and then he pulled out my dick and started stroking it. Well, one thing led to another, and before we were done, I had my hand around his solid prick and was pounding it the same way. I sure liked the way it felt when that hot juice came shooting out of my pecker, and we used to jerk each other off whenever we got a chance.

Then I found another buddy who wasn't satisfied with just massaging my iron, and when we got to fooling around, he took my pants and shorts all the way down. He said he'd show me a real thrill, and then he got down on his knees and started sucking my cock. That felt better than anything I'd ever felt before, and he kept right on working on it even after I told him I was going to come. He drank down every drop of that rich cream, and afterward he said he'd Frenched plenty of guys but that I delivered one of the best loads he'd ever had. Any time I wanted to go, he was ready to take it, and I kept him pretty busy!

I pulled a muscle during spring football in my senior year, so every day after practice the assistant coach would tape it for me. His name was Don and he was about twenty-five, and a damn nice guy. Well, one afternoon after I'd showered, I was lying on the table in the first-aid room with just a towel around me and Don was taping my knee, and suddenly I felt him slide his hand up my leg under the towel. I didn't know what to do, and then he was playing with my balls and doing things that made my big peter come to life. He said that he had watched me in the showers a lot and that he'd been waiting a long time to get to me. Then he went over and locked the door and pulled the blinds over the windows, and when he came back, he pulled the towel right off me. My tool was sticking straight up, and he grinned and said it was certainly a fine one. Then he bent over and started licking it with his tongue, just the big, pink head at first and then all over, and that made me shake like crazy. When he had it dripping wet, he began sucking it and playing with my nuts at the same time. I just lay there, and it sure was something to watch my meat slide in and out between his hot lips! I got awfully excited, and when I couldn't hold it any more, I grabbed his head and held it down there while I jammed my cannon into his throat and let it fire all it wanted to. He gulped it down, and when I stopped shooting, he went on licking for a long time. After that, I lay there resting while Don rubbed his hands all over my legs and arms and body, and I really felt great.

I liked Don an awful lot, and I guess he knew it. He was quite good-looking, and although I'd never seen him stripped, I knew he must be very well-built because he was quite athletic. It wasn't long before we were spending a lot of time together.

One Saturday night when my folks were out of town, Don invited me to stay over at his place. We had a lot of beer, and by bed-time, I was kind of drunk. When I went into the bedroom, Don was already stripped to his shorts, and he certainly looked fine! He had big, solid shoulders and arms, and his skin was very nicely tanned. His broad chest was covered with soft, dark hair, and his belly was flat and hard as a rock. He knew I was gassed so he helped me undress down to my shorts, and then he turned out the light and we climbed into bed together. It felt awfully good just to lie there with him next to me, and then he turned on his side and began running his hands over me slowly. Finally he got down to my skivvies, and he said we would both be more comfortable if we stripped all the way. He pulled off my shorts and then his own, and then he put his arms around me and held me tight. I liked the way it felt to lie up next to Don that way, and after a while, I got pretty excited. Don had me stretch out on my back, and he started running his lips and tongue all over me until his face was right in my crotch. My cock was real hard by this time, and he gave it a licking that really set me on fire, and then drank down all the juice I could give him. We just lay there for a while, and then Don pulled me over so my head was on his shoulder and I put one hand on his chest. I sure liked playing with the soft, curly hair that spread between his tits and ran down over his solid belly, and finally Don moved my hand right down between his legs. I had my first handful of real man-sized organs! I fooled with his big, slippery balls for a little, and then I wrapped my fingers around his rigid dick and stroked it some. Having that hot meat in my hand and hearing Don's excited breathing made me feel very strange, and the next thing I knew, I was on my knees between his legs staring at him.

There was something about seeing Don lying there naked that really got me, and I couldn't take my eyes off his huge pecker. It was quite thick and tall, and the pink bulb on the end of it was swollen and throbbing with hardness. Then, without a word, Don reached down and grabbed it, holding it up to me, and suddenly I was rubbing my lips over it and then my tongue. I heard him sigh and felt his rugged body quiver, and that made me want it all the more. I choked a couple of times because I wasn't used to having anything like that in my mouth, but once I got the hang of it, I did the best I could, and finally he held it all the way down my throat while I swallowed all the hot cream that came pouring from it. Gosh, what a drink I got!

Don and I had a wonderful time together, and we spend most of the next day in bed. I'd never known anyone as fine as Don, and he said he would get me a job at the camp where he was going to be life guard if I wanted to spend the summer with him. I sure did!

That was one summer I'll never forget! We had a little cabin all to ourselves, and we really had a ball! One night toward the end of summer, we were in the shower together, and I threw a rod while I was washing Don's back. It stuck right out between his legs, and finally he said it was time he showed me where to put it where it would feel best. We climbed into bed, and after he'd gotten me plenty worked up, he covered my meat with some kind of grease and rolled over on his hands and knees, telling me to slip it between his cheeks. He helped me work it into his hole, and I was afraid I'd come just from the excitement.

He had me start very slowly, and pretty soon I was pumping my dripping tool in and out of his sweet ass like crazy. What a sensation! I thought I'd go nuts before we both shot our loads, mine into his steaming hole and his all over my pounding hand! I had never felt anything as good as that, and Don gave me several more lessons before summer was over. One night he said he would like to get his prong into my rear but that he would wait until he was sure I was ready to try it. A couple of times he turned me on my stomach and fooled around with his fingers, but he said it would be easier for me if we waited until we got back to town and could get a little drunk first.

On the first night we were back in town, four of Don's friends came over for a drink. Chuck, Gene, Mike and Ed were all in their early twenties and athletic like Don, and we all had a good time together. They had brought a couple of bottles of whiskey, and we had quite a bit to drink. After a while, Chuck wanted Don to drive him somewhere, and as soon as they were gone, Gene said he would fix me a real drink. He gave me a glass half-full of whiskey with just a little water in it and sat down on the couch beside me while I drank it, and when I'd finished, I was feeling pretty high. He put one arm around my shoulders and told me to relax, and then he kissed me very hard on the mouth. I didn't know what to do, and then he kissed me again, and as he held me close, I could feel him unbuttoning my shirt all the way down.

Then Ed sat down on the other side of me, and pretty soon he was rubbing his hands up and down over my legs and crotch while Gene felt around inside my shirt. I got kind of scared because we were all getting worked up, and finally Gene said they would let me go if I would suck him off. I didn't know what else to do, so we all went into the bedroom, and Gene took off his clothes and lay down on the bed. He was husky and very well-built, and his prick stood up nice and hard from his hairy groin.

Ed had me strip to the waist so Gene could get a good feel, and then I knelt down on the bed between Gene's legs. I'd never tried taking anyone except Don, but once I got Gene's prong wet down, I didn't have any trouble working on it. He sure went wild, squirming and rolling around and yelling how much he liked it and how good it felt, and finally he unloaded a real hot blast right into my throat. Wow!!

Ed and Mike had been watching the whole show, and when Gene and I got up from the bed, Mike brought all four of us another drink. He said that he and Ed would be more comfortable if they took off their shirts, only when they stripped, they went all the way down to their shorts. They were both plenty big and rugged, and while I drank, Mike stepped up behind me and rubbed his palms over my butt steadily.

He said he had certainly enjoyed watching me in action, especially the way my ass had quivered and shook when Gene came, and feeling the thick, black, hair on his powerful chest rub against my back while he talked made me sort of nervous and excited. Suddenly he jammed both hands down inside the back of my pants and shorts and grabbed my cheeks. That scared me, and I tried to pull away, but he held on tight. Then he said that getting a handful of nice, young tail made him hotter than hell and that I would have to drop my pants so he could screw his tool into it, and when I told him I had never been fucked, he laughed and said that no one who spent a whole summer with Don could stay a virgin.

I finally got away from him and ran for the door, but he got there first and locked it, saying he was going to fuck me whether I wanted to or not. Then he jerked off his shorts and came after me naked, and I knew he meant business. He was bigger and stronger than I was, but I kept trying to fight him off until he yelled to Ed to help him.

Then they were both all over me, and I could feel them pulling my pants open and stripping them down over my legs. They ripped my shorts right off me, and then Mike stuck his hand between my legs from behind and grabbed my balls hard. I screamed with pain, and Mike said if I didn't spread my cheeks, he would cripple me and then screw me anyway.

I couldn't think of anything except the way my nuts hurt, and the next thing I knew, I was spread out face down across the bed. Ed was on one side holding my wrists while Gene was on the other side hanging onto my ankles, and then Mike got down on his knees between my legs. I felt him spread a lot of warm spit between my cheeks, and then his fingers were probing deeper and deeper until he was touching the lips of my asshole. I was awfully drunk, but I kept as tight as I could while he went on poking around, and then Ed laughed and said it was too bad I couldn't take it on my back because I would go out of my mind if I saw the solid ram Mike was getting ready to slam into me.

Finally Mike muttered that if I wouldn't open up enough to get reamed, he'd plough me without a warm-up, and then he pushed a huge piece of throbbing meat between my cheeks. I felt the smooth, solid head rub my hole steadily, and Mike said it was already dripping hard enough to give me a good lube job. I wouldn't relax those tight lips, and every time he jabbed that prong forward, it hurt a lot, and I begged him to let me go. At last, he cursed me for not letting him slide it in without a fight, and then he said he would have to dynamite me open.

Gene jerked my legs as far apart as he could, and Mike grabbed my cheeks and held them wide open as he pushed the tip of his pecker against my hole. I couldn't tighten up enough to stop him any more, and then I felt his huge flange ripping into me. It felt like he was tearing me apart, and I yelled and thrashed around like crazy until Ed jammed my head between his legs and held me there helpless.

The next thing I knew, Mike was lying flat against my back, and I could feel his potent hammer pulsating inside me. I heard Ed say that maybe I was a virgin because I was so tight and had put up such a fight, and Mike replied that it didn't make any difference now because he was going to fuck me until my trench was swamped with good, juicy cream. Then he began pumping his prong in and out slowly, and after the first couple of trips, it seemed to slide much easier. I was numb and dazed, and I don't remember much after that except the steady, jarring thrusts of Mike's pounding club as he drove it into me. At last I didn't think I could stand any more! I could hear Gene and Ed yelling to Mike to screw me harder, and Mike was grunting and gasping for breath, and then I was out of my mind as that rigid pole seemed to explode clear through me!

Then I was lying on the bed, and someone was cleaning me up with a damp cloth and wiping me dry with a towel. A few minutes later, Ed brought me a drink of whiskey, and while I sipped it, he peeled off his shorts and lay down beside me, playing with my balls. When I'd finished, he said that he wanted to shoot his wad into my tail, and when I begged him to leave me alone, he squeezed my nuts hard and told me to get up on my hands and knees.

I was too weak to fight any more so I did as he said, and then I felt him behind me, and his prick was pushing between my cheeks. He probed a little, saying that Mike had gotten me nice and loose, and then he told me to grit my teeth because the head of his cock was a lot bigger than Mike's.

Suddenly Gene called that Don was coming, and I yelled as hard as I could for help. Ed cursed and smashed his hot flange against my hole and drove just that huge knob inside as Don began pounding on the locked door. Ed pumped the head of his tool a little, making me groan because it was so big, and then he said, they might as well let Don see his buddy get fucked.

Gene opened the door, and Don came running in, yelling at Ed to let me go. Ed just laughed, and then he gave my balls a terrible twist and jammed his cock all the way into my aching asshole. I could hear my voice croak as I tried to scream, and I think I came just from the pain before everything went black.

After that, I vaguely remember being in the shower with Don and having him wash me all over, and later we were in bed together and he was holding me close to his warm nakedness. He said that I would feel better after a little rest, and I finally calmed down and drifted off to sleep.

I sure must have slept hard because when I woke up the next morning, I found Don's tool was buried in my ass, and he said he'd had it there most of the night. It sure felt a lot better than when Mike and Ed had had theirs in the same place!

CHAPTER SIX
ROUGH AND TOUGH

In its original form, *Rough and Tough* comes complete with very graphic illustrations on every page and the story is printed atop the illustrations. The pictures or drawings are done with painstaking detail.

Sado-masochism is a favorite subject for many erotic writers. Both the stories in this chapter deal exclusively with males who find themselves forced into sexual congress with sadistic partners. Generally, experts in the field of psychology and psychiatry contend that the masochist feels exonerated from blame inasmuch as he has been forced to commit the perversities he performs. He, in his own mind, does not hold himself responsible for his actions because they are actually done against his will. The so-called heterosexual male who allows himself to be fellated by a homosexual certainly does not consider himself as possessing homosexual tendencies; he did not actually participate in the affair, he convinces himself, he merely laid there and got "blowed".

* * * * * * *

I met Jake in one of L.A.'s many "gay" bars. It was crowded and he was sitting in a booth alone, drinking beer. He looked so much alone that I asked to join him. Readily, he consented, and we talked about various bars, the characters one met in them and so on.

At last he volunteered to tell me the story of his life. He was twenty-seven, and had been a school teacher in Iowa, but now was doing other work. He knew few people, and was not aggressive enough to make many friends. When I told him I was a writer, he brightened up at once and said: "Maybe you would care to write my life history?"

Hastily, I changed the subject by calling his attention to a "butch" and "fem" duo that were making mad love in a far booth. One glance was enough. "Women," he muttered. Then, "Please let me tell you about myself. I must tell someone!"

Well, I resigned myself, pegging him as another bar-room bore, ordered a double and told him to go ahead, but to be frank, blunt and have no fear of shocking me. Here is his curious story, word for word, without embellishments:

* * * * * * *

I had no sexual experiences until the age of sixteen, other than jacking off. I was shy with girls and never talked about sex with other boys. One day a neighbor boy of fourteen came down into the basement where I was stacking wood. The folks were away. He was big, tall and wore a leather jacket. Instinctively I was timid in his presence. He grabbed up an old tire tube and threw it around my shoulders. I recoiled, as the smell and feel of rubber always had been distasteful to me. I told him so. His eyes flashed and he seemed to relish the thought. Then he said, "So you don't like rubber, eh, Jake?"

He seized a small rope and in a flash, bound my arms to my sides, then my ankles. Next he threw me to the floor and twisted the inner tube around my neck until I thought I would choke. All the while he was calling me vile names, such as cocksucker, motherfucker, cuntlapper and so forth. He forced me to chew the inner tube and suck on it. Although I was in terror with aversion to the rubber, somehow I was thrilled by his brutal treatment. Suddenly he pulled out his large organ which was fully erect. "Jake," he said, "are you a good cocksucker?"

I told him I knew nothing of sex, but jacking off. He roared with laughter and told me I would have to learn sometime. Then, standing over my prostrate body, he masturbated all over my face and neck. After he left, I managed to untie myself and said nothing to anyone about the episode. For days I was not the same. I relived every moment and found that, degrading as it was, his torture thrilled me.

For many years after that I had no more sex whatever. I had left home and was teaching school in Milan, Iowa. One November night I was returning from a school entertainment quite late. Fate struck the second time. I was the last one on the bus, and it was bitter cold with snow falling. At last I noticed the driver, a Negro who was a big strapping fellow. He wore heavy boots and a tight leather jacket.

My heart gave a great leap because he reminded me so much of the neighbor boy who had abused me. I don't know why but my nerves tingled all through me. He turned from the wheel and asked my street. I told him the end of the line and then ten blocks further. He whistled and said, "Boy you can't walk that far in this snow! Tell you what, I'm turning this crate in the barn in twenty minutes, my car is there and I'll drive you home." I hesitated, as I noticed him taking quick looks at me from head to foot.

We got his car and he drove me home without much conversation. At the door of my apartment, I hesitated again, and then asked him in. Seated in my best chair, he asked about myself. I had some whiskey, although I seldom drink, and he gulped down a double shot like nothing.

At last he said, "Well, you've treated me nice, how about sucking me off?"

I didn't know what to say. He rose and pulled out a huge organ, almost erect, that stood out at least ten inches. He pulled me down on the sofa and presented the swollen weapon to my lips. I stammered, "I've never done that before. I'm sure you wouldn't enjoy it!"

Flexing his great arms and waving that grand tool he said,

"Suck me off, right now!" I began to protest, and he added, "If you don't, I'll tell every colored fellow I know where you live and they will come out here to have a good time with a nice fellow who will suck their pricks!"

Well, suddenly a new feeling came over me. Seeing that I had to do it, seemed to make a difference. I took it in my mouth and sucked! Twice I choked with the torrent of juice, but he held my head with his big hands and made me swallow every drop. I should have been filled with revulsion, but instead, a new, utterly foreign sensation went through me. He left right after that. Although I anxiously awaited his return, and possibly many others of his race, I never saw him again in my apartment. I did see him driving the bus, but he just said, "Hello!" as he did to everyone, and never mentioned visiting me.

The next episode did not occur for a year. I happened to be walking near the athletic field one night. There was a small cottage nearby where the football coach and a friend lived. I had always wondered about them, and why the coach didn't have a wife. Suddenly tonight he approached me, out of the shadows along with his friend and said: "Jake, what in the hell are you doing here—spying on us?"

I hastened to deny it, but Larkin and his friend insisted that I come into their house and talk for a while. They were very suspicious. Finally the coach insisted that I suck him off. After that I had to suck his boy friend off to prove that I was their friend. It was absurd, but I got a kick out of it.

Then Larkin wanted to stick his large prick into my behind. We had a big fuss, but finally he did and it was very painful at first. After he had it in, it soon gave me a new thrill; I went off with tremendous force, almost fainting from the pleasure, and I reveled in the fact that he was dominating me completely. I seemed to enjoy having someone be my master.

He was a big rugged fellow and he got a hell of a kick out of this also. Later I had to take on his boy friend, who was one of the football players, but by that time I was enjoying this abuse, and did not mind it at all. We spent the whole night in wild new adventures and the next day I was too exhausted to attend my classes. I had to telephone and say I was ill, but in the afternoon they left for football practice, and I went home to rest and get some sleep.

I was very eager to have more experiences, but there was no opportunity. Then my uncle prevailed upon me to come out west to Los Angeles. I found there were no teaching jobs available at that time, so I took a job in an office.

I rented a room in a Hollywood Hotel, and it was there that I met the frog-man! I was in the hall one night while on the way to my room. He was over six feet tall, with a mop of unruly, curling hair. I would guess his age at twenty-four, and he must have weighed 210. He wore a brown leather jacket and boots— that brought back memories to me—and I began to tremble with excitement.

He stopped right in front of me, and I smiled in recognition, as we had seen each other in the hotel on several occasions. I looked up into his suntanned rugged face. I smelled perspiration; his brow was wet with it. His gaze traveled over me from head to foot.

Then he said, "Say kid, how would you like to take a shower with me? I need someone to scrub my back." He grinned at me boyishly.

I was utterly amazed, but I followed him to his room and sat on the bed. Carelessly he undressed, and I could not take my eyes from his great body. He had a build like Atlas, or Mr. America. I undressed too and we stepped into the shower. The powerful muscles rippled under my hands. I even dropped the soap, I was so excited! I thought that he might want to have a sex party in the shower, but he restrained himself, or at least didn't suggest it. He scrubbed my back too, and I began to enjoy the affair more and more.

When we finished with the shower I helped dry him off with a rough towel, and could not keep from looking at his huge organ that was puffed up some and was pink. I dried it carefully, and then he rubbed it several times with his big hands. He spoke up then. "Kid, are you a good kisser—I sure need to get my gun off?"

I told him how little I knew of such things, but he would not listen, and was really aroused after making the first proposal and thus breaking the ice between us. With his mighty weapon half erect and swaying in front of him, he walked over to the closet and brought out a curious mask.

Now it was that I began to realize what his type of passion was: he liked to show off his brutal strength, and be dominating in sex. Next from a drawer came a pair of large rubber flippers, like shoes. He snapped the mask over his head and buckled on a heavy leather belt about his waist. "Now, kid," he said, "you are looking at a real live FROGMAN!"

"What's that?" I asked in astonished innocence, although I had heard of them.

"I swim and do things in the water that even a diver can't do! I learned it during the war, and now I'm working at it professionally on my own."

Suddenly he was upon me! He rubbed his now erect prick against my nude body as I lay back on the bed, and hugged me to him tightly, his hands feeling all over my body. The mask made this seem like being attacked by someone from another planet, and I was half frightened by his actions. He was a wild brute now, and he gloried in it. Grasping his big tool he ordered me to kiss it. I did without any hesitation, sucking on the throbbing head until he was squirming with delight.

He seized my organ and masturbated it roughly, until I went off all over his powerful thigh. "Lick that off!" he commanded, in a frenzy of lust. I managed to do so, while his hand was caressing my buttocks. Then he rubbed my rear. I never would have believed that bulging penis could enter without splitting me, but it did! We had three of four parties before that night was over. I never saw a fellow so wild for sex—he must not have had any for a long time—and his body just had to have it constantly.

I stayed in his apartment four or five days, and will never forget that experience. I lost track of how many times we had sex, and each time he would dress up in his "frogman" outfit, to show off, as that seemed to give him an added thrill—a perfect example of exhibitionism. He had meals sent up to us, and when he had to leave he would lock the door and make me promise that I would make no attempt to leave! Well, by that time I was so fascinated with him that I never wanted to leave. I would have done anything that he asked—and did, in our sex parties!

One night he returned in high spirits, saying he had a possible government job. So he stripped, and after I had given him his bath, he set up a card table and portable typewriter. Then he had me get down between his legs and give him a blow job while he was busy typing out his application. He thought this was great fun, saying: "You are an English teach and I may want to know how to spell a word!"

Every morning and night he made me suck him, and then he would screw me! Sometimes he would have me go off two or three times. I was about worn out!

The last night he was about to start in on me again when he heard footsteps in the hall—the clicking of a woman's high heels. "I know that gal," he whispered. "I've been waiting for her to get back in town." Seizing his slacks he dressed in a few moments. "You stay right here," he commanded. "Don't you leave. I'm going out and fuck her!" He left me to wonder what sort of maniac he really was!

Soon he was back in high spirits. Tearing off his clothes, he approached me with his half-erect weapon, which looked wet and slimy. "I just fucked that gal good, and now you are going to clean up my cock!" I protested, but he was simply nuts with sex passions. "It will be your first taste of pussy juice," he laughed. I nodded and went ahead with the job.

A little later the phone rang. "Answer it, but be careful what you say," he told me. It was my aunt, the clerk downstairs having transferred the call to this apartment. We talked for a long time, and she wanted me to come and live with her. My lover had another erection by this time, and while I was talking on the phone he was rubbing the big thing all over my face, tickling it into my ears and mouth between words, etc. The usual orgy went on most of the night. He shot his gun off time after time.

The next morning he said I would have to get along without him for a while, as he had to see about the government job. I went to my room and slept, as I was utterly exhausted. Next day I learned he had checked out, leaving another hotel address. I rushed there but he had not arrived. I've walked the streets looking for him for weeks—but I know he'll come back. Also I know another thing by now—I was completely his slave!

The apartment is a first floor and basement rear duplex, more or less isolated, which enters on a balcony staircase leading to a large sunken two-story living room with bedroom off the side rear.

When I arrived at eleven p.m. as ordered, the host informed me that the other M had backed out at the last minute, but that the other two S's had already arrived and were ready and impatient to get started. He met me at the door and immediately led me down into the side bedroom where, with no conversation but a few brief commands, and no preliminaries whatever, proceeded to strip me, doing it so quickly and roughly that he ripped my shirt and shorts so that I had to leave them there. In less than sixty seconds he had me standing before him start naked.

He quickly snapped a metal studded leather collar around my neck and another around my wrist, doubling my arms behind my head and fastening my wrist to collar with a small padlock. He put the key in his pocket. Thus tied, I was completely exposed and unable to resist or protect my body from head to toe. After an approving stare at his handiwork, he marched me out to the main room and stood me in front of the two other guys whom I'd never seen before.

One was over six feet, a husky built virile type about twenty-nine. His hairy chest and stomach showed through his open leather jacket, which with snug white briefs and ankle boots, were all he was wearing. The other was twenty-five or twenty-six but looked very rosy-cheeked and boyish, medium build and smooth blond body. He wore only a pair of very tight washed-out sailor pants, being nude well below his navel, and barefoot.

My host, in his early thirties, had on, at the beginning at least, more than anyone. He was dressed in complete motorcycle pants and cap with shirt, leather jacket and boots to match. Physically he was average, athletic physique, with an angular but attractive hard face resembling actor Wendell Corey somewhat.

Between these three, two total strangers, I was made to stand nude at attention with my legs spraddled wide apart while they proceeded to inspect and examine every inch of me at their pleasure. They slapped, prodded, pinched, and pulled the various parts of my body. The boyish one's fingernails—though not too long—were filed very sharp and he delighted in using them to scrape down my back and chest, to pinch and twist my nipples almost in two, to jab into my urethra hole after making my cock stiff, and to gouge it deep into my anus as well as my belly button and then screw his finger around inside at the same time snapping it out suddenly till it felt like my asshole or navel was being pulled inside out like an inverted finger on a rubber glove.

The big fellow did the same with his whole hand in my ass, compelling me to bend over with head to ground for his greater convenience. Although his nails were less sharp, his fingers were thick and strong and hurt just as much when he probed my groin muscles, yanked my genitals in his fist, twisted my tits, etc. Besides doing all these things too, the host also showed them how to pull out little tufts of my pubic hair while standing on my toes with his boots to prevent me from lifting my legs protectively. They continued making me kneel, bend, squat, stretch, etc., for about an hour.

Finally the other two were urging the host to start using special equipment. At first they left it to the host to initiate things, but they quickly caught on and joined in. He took full advantage of his power and position and promptly pushed me forward into the center of the room so he could have free arm swing. First wrapping the buckle end of a two inch wide black marine belt around his fist several times, he then stepped back several paces balancing his stance, and while I stood trembling naked at attention, he raised the long remaining strap high over his right shoulder and brought it whistling down to slash across my backside and buttocks, the end curling around to my belly where the hole perforations on the tip left blood pricks.

Stunned by the force, I let out a yelp. So he calmly stopped for a moment, made me fall to my knees, kiss his boots, remove them with my teeth, kiss his socks, tug them off, lick his feet, then stand in position again while he stuffed three sweaty socks, one of each guys, the others already being off, into my mouth as a gag.

Then he gave me another excruciating slash of the whipstrap. At the sudden sharp sting, I ran over behind the big black grand piano in the corner for protection, pleading in gurgles through my gag. My attempt to disobey clearly angered him. But, though his face was grim, he only commanded me through clenched teeth to, "Get back out here!" as he indicated dead center of the floor, He didn't move from his position and made no attempt to come after me.

But I knew from previous experience as well as the tone of his voice when he sternly repeated the four monosyllables that it was useless to resist. In his face you could see that he felt as host, leader and master that this was his absolute right and privilege. I walked back slowly and resignedly, while he stood with whip raised, ready!

The moment I reached the central area he began laying it on. For the next ten or fifteen minutes he disciplined me for daring to disobey him even briefly. I danced first on one foot and then on the other twisting and turning to no avail as he persistently plied the lash, adroitly avoiding danger spots such as head, kidneys, genitals, but fully covering my body till when his arms became temporarily tired at the end, I looked as though I had been tightly bound in flesh colored ribbons from shoulders to heels.

All the while the other two stood to one side eagerly enjoying it all, each anxiously waiting his own turn to give me the same treatment. Upon finishing, each made me drop to my knees at his feet, kiss the whip, kiss his hand and thank him for correcting me.

After all three had had their satisfaction in full this way and had left me shaking all over and my chest heaving for breath, I had about ten minutes respite to sink down on the piano stool while they were getting more equipment ready. Clearing a space on the floor, the big hirsute guy got out a large candle almost two inches in diameter and eight or nine inches long even after one end had been molded into a bullet headed nose. Having first dipped it into a stinging shaving astringent, he held a match underneath the base till wax puddled on the floor, then fixed the candle firmly upright in it.

He started off first this time as obviously this was his special trick that gave him kicks. He commanded me to come to him, then made me straddle over the candle and squat down onto it until it spiked into my ass hole. When I stopped half way down on it, pleading that I couldn't take it any further, he slowly but firmly pushed down on my shoulders until my buttocks touched the floor and the candle was agonizingly ramroded up into my rectum, the liniment burning fiercely.

While I was forced to remain in this painful crouching-sitting position, he then put the strong fingers of both his hands into my mouth like opened scissors stretching it wide, and warned me to keep it open. Standing before me, he shoved his enormous penis into it and began to piss, ordering me to swallow every drop. When he had finished, the host and cherub-cheeked one followed suit and since all had been drinking a lot of beer, I soon had a bloated belly full. Even after two of them thought themselves through pissing and had pulled out, they found they still had some left and finished by letting go in my face and all over my body until I was drenched and dripping as well. The husky fellow then made me kneel forward face down while he yanked the candle so suddenly I thought my whole guts were being torn out.

Before I even had a chance to stand up, the young fellow had grabbed me by the hair and dragged me half-stumbling, half-crawling across the room where the rug had been rolled back, and promptly pressed me face down flat onto the bare hardwood floor. The host and the other S helped him stretch my legs into a wide V and chain my ankles to opposite sturdy legs of the piano, and chain my wrists, which had been unfastened from the collar, to a pipe across the room. Finally my neck collar was locked to another chain, secured to the radiator diagonally opposite. Thus I was spread-eagled naked in the middle of the floor.

It was the blond boy's turn to take over this time. He uncoiled a cowboy bull whip about four and a half feet long. Next he stood far enough off to one side, took careful aim, paused a minute to gag me again, and this time with the big guy's dirty jockey shorts he'd taken off, then with expert precision, he proceeded to wield the whip up and down across my bare back, butt, and thighs while I moaned, flinched and strained. But I was too tightly leashed to be able to move more than an inch in any direction.

Though I struggled desperately to escape the constant steady stroke of the rawhide each time as it snaked through the air and snapped into my naked flesh, the boy's eyes glowed with the pleasure of his particular passion as he watched me squirm.

After what seemed an eternity, the big guy borrowed the bullwhip. He preferred to stand at my head, shoving the toe of his boot into my mouth as a gag instead. He laid on lengthwise down my back, planting my skin with welts. Fortunately for me, as I thought I might pass out, the host bypassed this one in favor of getting his own special rigging ready as he wanted to be able to work on my front side as well as my back.

The host let me into the bathroom and the others came in to watch and help him hold me under an ice cold shower till I was chattering and shivering all over. However, it did at least clean and revive me. The apple-cheeked one insisted on bending me over the sink to whack my bare behind with a sanded ping pong paddle he'd brought in with him.

He knew it stung twice as much when I was wet. This aroused lust in all three, so I was next led back to the living room where they all took off whatever little they still had on. They took turns lying out on the couch. The host was first. He made me kneel down in front of him while he held my chin up with his left hand, and ordered me to open my mouth. When I didn't open it quickly enough to please him, he brought the broad flat palm of his right hand down with a smarting slap first on my right and then on my left cheek. Then he leaped forward and spit directly into my mouth so I'd have plenty of saliva of his mixed with mine to give him a thorough tongue bath.

Lying out full length, face down, he first made me start by licking his toes, soles, heels, ankles, etc., and slowly working up his calves, thighs, and to his ass for a prolonged rimming, then up his back, shoulders, neck and in his ears. Upon which he turned over, exposing a throbbing erection that kept bobbing up and down against his belly. I was ordered to massage it with my fist while simultaneously I had to tongue down his Adam's apple, his pectorals, his arm pits, reaming his umbilical, abdomen, loins, crotch, testicles, and finally his hot prick.

All the while he smoked a cigarette, often flicking the ashes on any convenient part of my flesh, and drank beer from a can. The others also drank and smoked while they sat and relaxed till it was their turn to be serviced too. By the time I had satiated the whims of all three, I could still taste salt a long time after from their perspiration-drenched bodies and exciting male musk as they'd worked up quite a sweat during the previous activities. All stopped just short of ejaculation however, as they wanted to save themselves for the next S session that followed almost immediately after this semi-rest period.

Earlier, the host had rigged up two strong hooks tooled into beams set about five or six feet apart on the two story ceiling. Attached to them were metal pulleys and chains. He put leather ankle straps on me, snapped them onto chain ends while the other held me till he hoisted me up so I hung upside down with my legs spread in a wide V and my head was suspended about three feet above the floor. My wrist was again secured behind my neck to a collar. Of course I was completely nude.

They were feeling both high and hot by now and really used a free hand with me. A harness made of two metal clamps was clipped firmly onto each nipple until they almost bit through. The cords attached to them were pulled back under my arm pits. One guy tugged back hard on each side behind me, so my chest was curved back at the same time it thrust out my belly and loins in a forward arch at just about arm level of the host, who was standing in front of me with a long thin flexible but tough rattan rod.

He proceeded to severely flay my exposed stomach and crotch using my belly button as a bulls-eye. He climaxed it by manhandling my penis till it was standing out rigid, and then slipping a very tight rubber noose over my balls and all to help keep the base constricted and my cock turgid and erect while he gripped my genitals firmly in his left hand, slowly and deliberately skinned it way back and flayed the tender tip with rapid incessant close-in strokes of his right until I was beside myself. This only increased his pleasure and his efforts.

However, at last he stopped and the other shifted around front to pull the cords forward so this time my bared bottom and thighs were forced sharply out behind for the host to rain blows upon. He wound up by flailing the rattan straight down in between my buttocks and my super-sensitive anus, my legs being stretched so wide apart, I couldn't even tense my sphincter muscle to soften the sharp stinging cuts of the cord as he brought it down again, and again, and again.

When he saw how glowing red and sore I was, it excited him to stick the thick candle into it upright and then light the wick on top, letting the hot wax drip steadily down into my crotch as well as trickle on down my torso. The candle burned down so close it felt as if a hot poker were searing my ass hole before they finally snuffed it out.

Then no longer able to contain himself, he told the other two to relax the cords so I hung straight down. Going around front, he rammed his already drooling cock into my mouth to moisten it up, and then withdrew it, went around back to my rear, lowered pulleys till my ass was level with his prick and drove it in and out of my ass until he came in a terrific charge flooding inside of me.

Without relief the big one and the boyish one in turn subjected me to the same torture, except they also bastinadoed the soles of my bare feet till they seemed on fire, my toes curling and nerves jumping. But even then I was not let down, for, by the time the third was through, the host was ready to shoot another load—this time down my throat. The others too exercised the same privilege before I was finally released after being jerked off so it splattered and ran all down my belly, chest and face, where each guy rubbed it in with the palm of his hand sticking their sweaty sticky fingers in my mouth one at a time to make me lick them off. Luckily this was my last night before going home as it was 5:30 a.m. by the time I was released, exhausted.

CHAPTER SEVEN
FACE ON THE FLOOR; OR, A MID-SEMEN'S NIGHT'S DREAM

This particular piece is perhaps the most typical example of the erotic story. It offers little in the way of genuine realism, literary value, or character development. It brings us back to that familiar theme, the introduction to homosexual sex, with immediate versatility, satisfaction, and lack of guilt or complications. It presents numerous depictions of genitalia, each penis larger than the next. The individuals are virtually insatiable. One's head fairly swims trying to differentiate between the various characters participating in the orgies—who is doing what to whom? But these are questions that do not generally concern the reader of such material, nor need they concern the more scholarly student either, for the significance lies in the acts performed, and the gusto with which they are accomplished. The very lack of character development and individuality is important and significant. The persons in these narratives have been reduced to so many penises, various bodies (and here the characters do differ and are described in detail) and numerous positions for fornication.

In only one respect does this one differ from countless other such stories—its lengthy title and profuse illustrations which accompanied the original.

* * * * * * *

I.

While taking a shower in the college gym, Alan and Kevin had been chatting about this and that when Alan popped up, "Say, Kevin, you are built like a Greek Adonis. Have you ever thought of making it pay off?"

"What the hell are you talking about? Sell my dauber by the inch?"

"No, ya jerk! I mean posing. Robin Stark, the photographer, is always looking for new material and you are just his meat. Curt, Greg, and me hang out down there two or three afternoons a week. Not only do we get a few dollars, but a lot of fun besides!"

"I'm afraid I couldn't take it. My rod swells every time I think about being nude in front of others. See?" By this time, Kevin's shining shaft was inching out. The foreskin was rolling back slowly and full eight inches of firm gristle bobbed at right angles from his ample balls. The column was a pink-white and very chunky and firm. The glans was a rose color and a most appealing sight. Kevin was eager, for his wand throbbed and the eye in the end seemed to be open and begging for attention.

Alan couldn't help but respond in a like manner, and out of his almost silver snatch bounded a man-sized, roaring hard-on, eager for action. "You've got a hell of a lot of meat for your age. Don't tell me you belong to the club too."

"Club?"

"Yeah, gay boys."

"Are you too?"

"Sure, Curt, Greg, and I have a whirl damn near every night. And Robin-wellllll. That Stark has ideas that would make Mr. Kinsey blush. His posing sessions are little less than orgies, and at a buck an hour. Yeah, a buck and a FUCK an hour. And if I weren't afraid of someone coming in, I'd like to grind my nose into that red nest of yours and let my throat muscles milk your cream supply right now."

"Would you really? I've always wanted to be blown, but I've been too bashful. I get all hot in the shower or watching the boys in the pool and then I have to fist fuck to get it to lie down so that I can go to sleep."

"Don't waste that love soup on a hand job. Give me a whistle, I'm always available for a load of spunk. Say, we'd better get to class. Why don't you stop in at Robin's this afternoon and see if you can't join the rest of us tomorrow? Saturday, we usually have an all-day spree and Robin has some special shots he wants to do tomorrow, with daisy chains, you know how it is—the more the merrier."

"No, I don't know how it is, but I think I'm about to learn, and my prick seems to be bursting with enthusiasm." Alan couldn't resist the temptation to heft Kevin's balls and to move his hand up and down the shaft a couple of times, hooding and unhooding a very hot, pulsing knob. Alan licked off the first beads of come and it tasted like nectar. "Mmm, I hope there's more where that came from. I'm getting thirsty."

It was now three o'clock and Kevin was approaching Stark's studio. Alan had assured him that one look at his flaming red hair and his physique and Robin would hire him on the spot, but Kevin wanted to be sure, so he was wearing his skin-tight Levi's and had squeezed his equipment down his left leg. His beautifully packed bummy snuggled into the jeans and bulged invitingly. Kevin had pulled back the foreskin of his flaccid cock as he dressed so that it would appear longer and make a pleasant five-inch bulge down his pant leg. Kevin always had a great deal of difficulty getting into this pair, and to sit down almost cut his basket in two, and by the time he was ready to peel out of them the friction of the cloth on his skinned wang had him hot for pumping his wad off. The anticipation of his "COMING OUT PARTY" however, had him aglow and he needed no additional urges to keep his dick semi-hard all day since his chat with Alan.

His eight-inch hard-on was now trying to stick out at an angle and was just about to burst the seams of his jeans.

Kevin was starting to get cold feet as he reached the studio door. Then he saw a shot of Alan hanging on the studio wall and though his gorgeous nuts and prick were half-hidden in a wisp of cloth, he mentally undressed Alan and recalled that pulsing shaft he had so wanted to suck earlier in the day. His hand was groping his hot tool and patting the tented material. By now he had unconsciously entered the waiting room and was entranced by Alan's blond beauty when he was brought down to earth by a male voice. "Well hello, Red, whose dream did you just step out of?"

Kevin turned about and faced Robin Stark, a bit nonplussed and with a very flushed face. Robin could easily have been his own model. He wore an outfit that could only be classed as a prick-teaser. The shirt was filmy and was open to the waist to reveal a full masculine chest of black hair and powerful shoulders tapering to a tiny waist. Black tailored denim slacks merely served to accentuate his full basket and show off his tight muscular ass to its best advantage. "What can I do for you?" What he would like to do was suggested by the growing shaft that was inching its way up his fly. Robin adjusted it in his pants so that pretty boy wouldn't miss the fact that he had hot nuts.

Kevin tried not to look at his crotch, but it was sort of hypnotizing. His whole mind was on sex and somehow he came out with, "Alan Spencer suggested that I see you about a posing job. He said that maybe you could use another boy tomorrow. Oh, I'm Kevin Moore."

"I never buy a package until I see what's inside. Come into the studio and strip and let me have a look."

Kevin was scared. His cock was fiery hot and beating down his leg. Golly, he was going to be embarrassed to show off a stiff rail. Robin relaxed in a leather hassock and Kevin shed his shirt, loafers, socks, and started to unzip his fly. No underwear hid Robin's view of the flaming red snatch as Kevin labored diligently to strip off the jeans in rapid order. Kevin turned his back and Robin had to put his hand on his own crotch, for that handsome ass set him on edge, and his own level staff rose stiff and hard against his pants.

As Kevin bent over to pull off the Levi's, his enticing pucker hole with its halo of red fur had Robin hot as hell. What a sight greeted Robin's eyes: Kevin stood facing him, his legs about a foot and a half apart, as though stanced for a royal fuck, and his joy stick was stretched to the fullest-dripping a bit from excitement, his pink balls nested tight to the rest of his cock and the bar itself was pointed skyward and twitching with every heartbeat, ready for action.

"Oh, boy, bring that lovely body over here where I can really get a good look!"

As Kevin approached, his eight inches of life bobbed up and down—down from sheer weight and up from passion. Robin put his arms about Kevin and his palms cupped the firm cheeks of his ass. "I hope you don't mind, but I'm a cock-sucker from way back and mean to give that delectable piece of meat the blowing it deserves."

His mouth engulfed Kevin's rod right to the nuts as Kevin gasped. Just as quickly he extracted the glistening beauty. "God, man, you are good enough to eat and as you can see, I'm hungry!" With that he ripped open his own fly and out popped a better than eight inch prick, but one that was very slim and curved upward like a cutlass. Robin continued chewing away at the squirming cock and thrills shooting through Kevin built rapidly to a climax. Kevin was too hot, however, for as Robin relaxed for a moment to kick off his slacks, Kevin's ass stiffened, every muscle quivered, and crushing Robin's head into his red curls, he poured out what seemed like a pint of come. It shot in thick spurts all over Robin's face and hair, and Robin was able to catch only a few blobs of the hot cream as it erupted from the beating penis. Robin's long eager tongue worked rapidly to catch the cascading tears as they rolled down Kevin's quivering testicles. "Gee, I'm sorry sir, I guess I was too hot. I'm afraid I shot my gunk all over you." His monster was still dripping.

"I have a standing rule. Everyone cleans up his own mess, so come lick off this discharge." Kevin's tongue got busy. This was the first semen he had ever tasted and ironically, it was his own, but it tasted so rich and heavy. His lips met Robin's and their tongues became lost in one another. The boys were now standing and were hugged into each other's arms. Kevin was taller. He had his legs apart slightly and had butted his wet, soggy snatch into Robin's. Robin's pulsing poker was purple with passion and pleading for pleasure.

As they kidded around, Robin began to hump his ass and grind his turgid pole into Kevin's groin. His actions were animal inspired, and soon he was rubbing his prick along Kevin's stomach, the crimson hairs tickling his bursting glans as it skinned and recapped, riding up and down his belly.

Robin began to hump his tail actively and his shoves became faster and faster and his kisses hotter and more brutal. Suddenly, Robin began to pant as he drove his tongue deep into Kevin and clung to him for dear life. His twitching rear and moans revealed that he was pouring out a shower of semen all over Kevin and he continued to rub in the slimy mess he had made. His body squirmed and wiggled and slid up and down Kevin as his spurting cock added more and more lubrication. When finally the supply became exhausted, Robin dropped to his knees and licked, kissed and sucked every spend on Kevin's wet body. His large mouth engulfed the flaccid cock and then he tried to suck in the sack of balls, but his mouth could only get one ball in at a time. He seemed in a trance as he licked and sucked more and more of Kevin's beautiful equipment.

Kevin's cock was starting to swell again. Robin took the tip of his warm mouth and twirled his tongue around the neck of the glans and tried to force his pointed tongue into the tiny hole. Kevin squirmed a bit as Robin ran his fingers through the thick red curls and played with the balls as his teeth held tight to the knob. He shook his head a bit, jiggling Kevin's balls about and completing the job of turning his handsome model's limp hunk of flesh into a ready shaft of gristle. "Better save that red-header for tomorrow. When these boys get going on you, your old leg won't rise for a week."

"Then I'm hired?"

"To tell the truth, I'd hire you just to get the opportunity to open your fly. By the way, how are you at fucking? My ass is twitching for a taste of your eight-incher."

"Well, I was a virgin until a few minutes ago, but I'm willing to try anything. I'd love to feel your wand up my butt. It's so long and slim."

"I've browned a lot of asses with it. Guess it was whittled down for comfort on the chocolate speedway because all my boys seem to beg for it that way. Turn around a bit." Robin parted Kevin's pink cheeks and ran his tongue around the pucker hole and drove it in. His tongue fell in love with the rose colored ass-hole. Quickly he closed his eyes and pressed his lips on the delicate little mouth which convulsively contracted and distended. Kevin wiggled from delight, for between kisses, the tickling tongue of his friend knew how to caress so gently the most sensitive spot.

"Holy Cow! That's too much. Please, PLEASE, OH, OH, don't stop. OH, OH, how wonderful that feels. Fuck me-FUCK ME-FUCK-FUCK-FUCK-shove that cock of yours UP-OH-PLEASE, I can't take it-OH-OOOH-IT HURTS-shove-harder-HARDER-OH, it's killing me. OH STOP-NOOO, DONT STOP! Grind your balls deep into me. OH, ROBIN!"

The big burning marauder of Robin's had worked its way through the portal of his hot ass like a well-oiled drive shaft. Then he began undulating to and fro. Forward and backward. Throbbing, quivering. Kevin tried to gauge the drive of the rigid hammer but Robin continued to go in and out, sideways— A long pull out—a jab in—a twist a little to the side—a stop—move slowly—a series of rapid, long, hard thrusts. His curved rod went into the hungry opening smoothly, up to the hilt. Now he developed a delicious cork-screwing motion. "OH GOD, I'M COMING!" His convulsive motions were very powerful. He groaned in his ecstasy.

"Relax kid, so am I." By now Kevin was spurting a load of hot come all over the room and Robin was locked in that sweet tangle, molded over Kevin's body and his arms about that gorgeous belly. Robin's slim prick was buried to the root in his partner's rectum and semen was oozing out of the love passage around his shaft and running over his snatch and sack of nuts which hung full and rounded, though just drained. "TAKE THAT, and THAT, and THAT, YOU BEAUTIFUL THING YOU!" As Robin buried his slowly shrinking tool into that eager rear. His hands now cupped Kevin's exhausted handle and massaged the remaining spend into his warm curls.

"We'd better shower and dress before I get the idea to inject that thick club of yours in my genii's eye. Golly, but you'd be an assfull, you know that? Bet you'd stretch a guy enough so he'd feel that plug up there for a week."

"Tomorrow? Your body sets me on fire—SEE—I'm damn near hard again!" His hickories were huge and pendulous, and he had a most soliciting prick.

II.

Saturday morning came and Kevin hurried to Robin's studio. The same jeans held his body in bounds and his eager sex organ was already giving him problems. The muscle between his legs was throbbing in eager erectness, already rock hard, tingling, and bulging out his fly. Kevin had been so excited as he dressed that he couldn't get into his jeans the usual way, so he had to hold in his stomach, press his shaft flat against it and zip up with caution to avoid meshing his red curls and pink flesh in the zipper.

Alan, Curt and Greg were sitting in the reception room as he entered.

"GIRLS," piped Greg, "GET a load of that BASKET. Honey, come sit by me. I have ten little fingers and ten tiny toes that are just aching for an early morning grope of a big piece of meat. Say, and it's all his, TOO! Nothing more disappointing than a sneak grope into a bursting crotch, only to find it padded with a pair of socks, but this is the MC COY! Alan says that you sport a full eight inches that's thick enough to choke a horse—and it's green timber too."

"It was green timber," chimed in Alan. "Remember, he got the job, so for sure, Robin drained his crankcase at least twice... RIGHT? And from the gingerly way he walks, it's for sure he got the full treatment up his tail. I could feel that plug between my legs for damn near a fucking week."

They all knew Robin's specialty too well. Greg took Kevin's hand and moved it his groin. "Here, have a feel—no sense being bashful! I'm hot and eager as you are."

Kevin was new at the game but it was fun and his eager hands played with Greg's muscular gun while his own was on fire from the fingers that tickled his bulging balls and prick. Curt seemed oblivious as to what was going on.

"What ails you, big boy?" asked Alan.

"Well, showering this morning I got to thinking back to last night, and I got so hot I had to suck off to get into my slacks and that always poops me."

"Yeah, Kevin, this Curt is some cocksman—he's got the longest stabber in town and he can suck off his own hard-on, so no fist fucks for him. He just rolls into his own hot lips and blows his own wad. He'll put on an exhibition later. He loves to show it off."

"Aw, shut up. You're just jealous."

"You're damn right I'm jealous! If I had eleven inches instead of seven, I'd walk down Main Street with it bobbing all the time. Well, we're all envious."

"Where's Robin?" asked Kevin.

"I don't know, but why wait out here? Let's go in and get out of these duds and into our G-strings."

"Anyone got an extra?" piped up Kevin. "All I've got is an athletic supporter."

"Large size, no doubt," said Greg. "I've got a dozen, though I doubt if they will hold. You're hung, man!"

The four boys went into the studio and discovered the place

was not empty. On the divan Robin used for posing shots ordinarily, was a handsome hulk of a man, flat on his back, his heels up over his head and his buttocks spread wide, his turgid penis drooling with come. Robin was on top pumping a steady stream of pulsing prick. His balls swung loose and slapped at pretty boy's butt with each forward thrust. Pretty boy was pouting like a fountain and Greg lost no time in joining the happy twosome and clamping his eager lips over the tip to catch every drop of come from his frantic spasm. Kevin was intrigued by anything sexual, so he stood by Greg watching every quiver. Greg then turned to Kevin and kissed him, slipping part of the hot, salty discharge into his mouth.

"Share and share alike, that's my motto."

Robin was in the process of shooting charge after charge from his cannon into the quivering body before him. His moans, plus the thrusts of his well-tanned ass, set all the boys on edge. Greg was a real sex hound, for as Robin's prong plunked out of his buddy, he was down on the floor licking up every drop of gism that oozed out of the bung hole. Robin pulled up his slacks that hung about his knees and massaged the spunk on his rod and balls into his nest and buttoned up. "Boys, this is Dien, my latest model. He just passed his entrance exams."

There was a general round of friendly exchanges and the boys didn't miss the opportunity to heft his balls and to stroke and peel back his drooping cock. Greg stood behind Dien and his hot equipment tented his slacks out fiercely. He rubbed the bulge into Dien's sweaty ass. Dien was as dark as Alan was light, from the mattress of hair on his chest to the thick jet black fuzz about his crotch, and his skin was a mellow brown except for a small triangle about his groin, and a line up the rear that showed that most of the ass had gotten full treatment from the sun. What a tease that butt had been all summer on the beach.

"Okay now, we've got to get some work done before we play. Strip and get into your posing straps. I've got to meet a deadline for the magazine. Some group shots and new catalogue of singles. Then something different. Any of you who want to go along with it—we're going to make a stag movie—lots of lovely sex—the hotter and more depraved the better. Also we have to make some still shots for the movie. So hold your fucking around for cameras."

By now all the boys were nude and slipping into wisps of this and that. Robin adjusted his cock and nuts in his jeans and slipped into a shirt. Greg tossed Kevin a very flimsy mesh job. "Try this for size."

Curt was wearing a completely transparent nylon job. His basket was tremendous and his straps were all especially made with sides doubly reinforced with elastic. His sack of balls was full, and creasing wrinkles could be seen through the sheer material. Limp, his dong was still longer than most when erect, so about seven inches of chunky meat was confined behind the film. The circumcised head was molded over the knockers and the whole effect was enough to give anyone an erection looking at it from any angle. Robin liked lots of hair, so Curt wore his strap low enough to show a whole inch of pubic hair over the top of the jock, and he let the fur on his nuts peek out along the side.

Alan wore a standard strap but his pecker was a bit too full of life for the moment, and the strap tented to the limit and actually covered nothing. It was slowly getting soft and Alan was adjusting the cloth. His hair was so light that the thick silver mat hardly showed. Alan squealed as he pulled the elastic through his ass crease to make the front as small as possible. He pulled it down enough so that half of his semi-inflated blob of flesh showed and the top of the balls peeked over the chartreuse patch.

Greg's mesh job formed around his tool and revealed every outline of his well-packed basket. With so much cream in his belly so early in the morning, his prick was throbbing and the strap had to be adjusted very tight to force his fully distended joy stick downward. Greg was in agony, but he knew that the stiffness would quiet down a bit. The elasticized material clung to every curve of his tool and in profile he showed off to be a very hot number.

Dien had little trouble covering his privates, for his relaxed cock and balls shrunk up very small never hinting that he had a good family-sized stabber six and a half inches. A large sticky wet spot in the center of his cock showed that his dabber still oozed from his recent orgasm.

Poor Kevin was having a real problem. His knockers were encased in the jock strap but his erection was so rigid that he couldn't press it down, and a full six inches showed above the strap, throbbing on his belly.

"Ready, boys, Curt and Greg, front and center." Robin shot a series of poses-wrestling, muscleboy, playful shots. "Curt, relax against that pillar and puff up your snatch a bit. It has settled down between your legs. Let's show all the sex we can in this one." Curt pulled the jock forward a bit and the elastic between his ass gave a bit so as to bulge his treasures out. Curt made a tremendous profile—his balls riding high and the full seven inches of prong in all its majesty curved over his testicles, every detail of his peeled dong visible to the camera. "Okay, Greg, kneel at his feet and put your hands on his thighs. Now look up at that pretty basket and show the camera that you are pleading for a chance to blow that horn."

"GOD DAMN YOU, Greg, quit," said Curt. "Every time I get a new nylon cock cover, this bastard bites my snatch and makes runs. These teasers cost three bucks and I have to fuck the fag who makes 'em."

"You should complain. How many bung holes are there that can take that ass club of yours? You poor, poor, baby— Greggie'll kiss it and make it better."

"The HELL you will, it's starting to squirm in my nest already."

"Spread your legs a bit there, Greg, let's see more of that crack in your ass. OOPS, that's too much. Mustn't show the tunnel of love. Just enough to make the fairy who buys these shots wish you had opened wider."

Greg and Curt did a series together showing off both baskets to the fullest. "I guess that's enough of you two." Greg couldn't resist the temptation to snap the elastic down over Curt's curls and to run his finger up and down the rapidly tumefying penis. "Please don't. You know once I get hard-on I can't get it down without a blow job, and I'm pooped. I picked up a sailor last night and we met behind the stadium. He brought along five buddies to see my act and it ended up with each of them trying to blow my wad. I did give up four times though and fucked one of the dolls right to the hilt. Now, I'm really a gagged out faggot."

"Okay hon," and Greg snapped the cozy cover over the bud with the sting of a bull whip.

"I'LL KILL YOU, Greg, SO HELP ME. I'll run every inch of my eleven inch toad stabber up your bung hole and you won't sit down for a month.... THAT'S a promise, hear? I've wanted to ream your ass and you're asking for it."

III.

Next *series—Dien the Dark and Alan the Light.* Dien was a ballet dancer, so he went through various poses showing Alan how to stand and how to hold his body. "Is ballet as sexy as it looks?" asked Alan. "I mean, are all the boys cocksuckers?"

"Well, I once met one who was strictly trade, but he's the only one who ever said no to my stiff cock. These outfits get us so riled up that there is always someone doing someone in the dressing room or in the wash room. After every rehearsal there is always a mad daisy chain. Our ballet master says that sucking makes the cock and balls grow larger, and he likes big bulges in those tights, so it is usually all suck and no fuck."

Alan's skimpy patch just about held his privates. The full and heavy hickories were half-exposed by the thin strap and so much silver fuzz stuck out all around the jock that it looked like a fur border. "Stand with one leg forward so that the tease area shows, Alan. Now throw Dien up on your shoulder so that his meat would be right in your mouth if your head were turned. YES, like that. Try it out. Okay, see, your nose is right into the belly and your tongue could easily lick his dong."

"Oh, Geeee, ALAN, DONT DO THAT! I'm too assy. It excites me too much."

"WHAT are you doing?"

"Just running my fingers along the crease in his beautiful rear. He feels so soft and sexy in there and it doesn't show in the picture."

"No, and it makes Dien look real lewd and as though he is thrilled by the prospect of your carrying him off to be fucked to a frazzle."

Dien had to take it and his basket swelled a bit, showing his excitement, as Alan shoved a finger deep into Dien's butt as the camera clicked and another lecherous shot was made. The second the shutter closed, Alan pulled Dien's jock aside and took his half-hard wand into his mouth. What a lustful scene the camera missed!

"Okay, Kevin, you're next."

Alan still held Dien over his hard shoulder, fingers caressing his little ass and his lips and cheeks were sucking for all they were worth on his rapidly erecting rod. "Quit fucking around, Alan. We'll have a break soon and you'll have plenty of time to blow every horn in sight, including mine."

Alan let Dien down and his mighty weapon, half-erect, swayed in front of him. One of the boys had turned on the stereo and Dien began to move his body to the rhythm of the music. His balls flipped from thigh to thigh and the half-hard prick jumped and wiggled with his every move and slapped against his belly and thighs as his movements became more active. "WOW...wouldn't ballet be sexy if the dancers were nude?" exclaimed Alan.

"Drop in on a rehearsal and find out," and Dien slipped his stiff behind a bit of silk before it got really uncontrollable. "Can't you get it down, Kev? That shot will never get through the mails."

Kevin was still sporting a rail inches above his flimsy patch. "I've tried thinking about everything but sex, but everything here is so sexy that my meat just gets harder and bigger and hotter. Maybe I'd better jerk it off," and his hand began to stroke the end of the protruding prick.

"Waste that masterpiece! I'd die first," added Greg. "No, we'll take a rear view or so and keep that beauty a secret. Take off your strap and relax a minute." His balls fell out so easily and his eight inches stood out very proudly from his flaming hair, towering outward. As his passion rose, the balls could be seen creeping closer and closer to the stiff and pulsing shaft. "Turn back, facing the wall, Kevin. Now, hold your legs tightly together and buck your hips forward a bit and your head back as though you just sent the final thrust into a real tight bung. Show a bit of that wonderful agony from your love muscle spurting its nectar at the climax of a furious browning. Now, another— Squat down a bit—golly, your cheeks open up so seductively— glad your pucker hole is pink, for it blends with the crease and I won't have to touch it up. Curt, slip off your strap and get behind Kevin. We'll take a three-quarter view of your rear, looking over Kevin's shoulder."

In a flick, Curt was nude and eleven inches was in full majesty, wobbling from side to side as he walked up to the platform. His was one of the biggest damned prongs anyone had ever clapped an eye on, and Curt was proud of it. He patted his belly, making his cock bob up and down. His nuts were starting to ache and for sure he had to have his kicks soon or he'd burst. "How does that feel, Kevin?" He shoved his full distended eager wand between Kevin's spread legs.

Kevin squeezed his thighs tight as an answer, and played with the knob that projected between his own balls. Curt was ready, for his cock was drooling and Kevin massaged the come into the fiery purple tip. Priapus himself must have furnished his tool. It was ready to burst with voluptuous juice and Curt started eager breathing.

"Hey...tease...that's enough of that!" Curt drew back a foot and parted Kevin's buttocks and pointed his knob at the target. From the camera angle the near foot-long prong didn't show.

The love weapon was more eager than ever before. It seemed to drill deep into this sheath. His stout moist rod had grown really hot in the oven between his legs. Instinctively, he began to rub his tool lustfully and passionately on the ass cheeks and on the narrow slit. His impatient stiff surged strongly upward.

"Mind if I take your measurements, beautiful?" whispered Curt. "I've got to ride that ass of yours." His whole body shook and his taut posterior quivered.

Robin had seen nothing of this as he was setting up his camera. "Hey, Kevin, move a little closer to Curt." Only one way was this possible, so Curt quickly ducked down to Kevin's all-encompassing ass and planted a good bit of saliva on the hole and added a bit of his immense quivering dong. He prodded his cock along the length of this teasing ass until he found the entrance to his love passage. He poked the head in all-knowingly, and paused. In a flash, he drove six inches up Kevin's equally hot, moist chasm of love. Kevin jerked forward, letting out a blood-curdling scream. "CHRIST...! WHAT DO YOU THINK THIS IS? THE HOLLAND TUNNEL?"

"You love it and know you do," said Curt, screwing his hips and butt around, inching deeper and deeper, ramming it brutally into Kevin. He wiggled his body from side to side working like a piston rod. As he moved back, the light picked up the thick shaft, wet and shiny. Below it, two round balls swung as his body moved. At this stage, a generous half of his organ was left outside the inhospitable portal.

"FOR GOD'S SAKE...STOP HIMMM...I CAN'T TAKE THAT...Ohhhh...I CAN'T, HE'S SPLITTING ME IN TWO!"

Kevin started to really cry but Curt merely pulled on Kevin's hips and thrust savage heaves into his tail. By now the heavy balls of Curt were slapping a very pink ass and his groin was matted on Kevin's buttocks. That incredibly big, almost bursting organ, was jammed into the slippery confines of his bung, stretching it to the limit. This savage rape had caught all the boys as a surprise and Robin was rapidly taking "action" shots while Dien and Greg, and Alan awed and oohed, and handled their own straining pricks and tossed off the tiny confining materials. Each sported enormously rigid hard-ons as they watched in satisfied excitement. Curt never let up for a moment and began to shove harder, grinding every inch of his proud plunger balls deep. Kevin squealed and squirmed and he was now feeling the thrill, "FUCK...FUCK...FUCK HARDER... OHHH, IT'S SO WONDERFUL!"

Curt began long, slow, steady motions in and out, fucking intensely. Curt held to his hips as his cock slid in and out of the tunnel of love.

Greg let go of his own jerking pecker for a moment and it slapped against his stomach. He darted for the platform with his balls swinging all over his snatch and his aching shaft clutched to his belly. Kevin felt a breath between his thighs and the next moment a warm mouth was clamped there. Greg couldn't resist the chance to go down on Kevin's leaping love stick. "Fellatio, here I come!"

In a second, Kevin's eight inches of drooling muscle disappeared down his gullet. What a masterpiece of love! In the moist cave it started to grow stiffer and harder and longer. "Oh, suck... blow me, quick!"

Curt gradually began slow easy strokes as Kevin loosened and tightened his loins. Wild desire began to take over on both boys and suddenly they both reached a tremendous climax. Their bodies trembled in ecstatic bliss as Curt pumped his hot cloudburst of liquid love into his partner and Kevin spewed forth his juice into Greg's eager mouth, treating his friend to his favorite liquor. Kevin let out a long drawn out groan as he spent, "AAAAAAaaaaa." His whole body vibrated with the force of his orgasm. Curt's gorgeous bulk was making a few spasmodic jerks as his juices flooded Kevin's intestines. The unremitting waves of ardent lust in their youthful bodies were almost more than they could endure, and the gasps and moans of pleasure set the whole studio on edge.

Greg choked from the torrent of seed, but Kevin held Greg's head tight to his crotch and made him swallow every drop that didn't seep out around the sucking lips. Curt gradually extracted his spent tool from Kevin's rear with a shudder of delight at the final good-bye squeeze it gave him. He rolled over on his side and patted his stomach contentedly.

Robin could see for sure that now was the time for a break and a wild melee. Besides, his balls ached he was so hot, and his cock actually hurt because it was pressed so hard against his zippered crotch.

Dien had been standing next to Alan while Curt rode Kevin's ass to a frazzle, and his attention was diverted away every so often as Alan's pink-white shaft bobbed up and down and the crimson glans crept out the prepuce and swelled to a size out of proportion to his average length shaft. At the base of his thighs, this club-like object stuck out at right angles. His silver snatch made Dien drool and Robin shouted, "BREAK!"

Dien faced Alan and pushed his rearing equipment into Alan's hand. "See how dark mine is and light yours is?" He was undulating his hips and their balls were caressing each other but both cocks were straining and lay along their bellies. "Mind if I taste, Alan?"

For an answer, Alan reclined on the nearby couch and held his tool and balls in both hands. "Trade you even!"

Dien's nuts were so tight and painful he could hardly walk, so he crawled into the saddle and in a moment, a 69 was in full swing. Dien was kneeling above Alan and his black head was lost between Alan's white thighs. His own hot, dripping meat was hanging over Alan's mouth, his tongue reaching out playfully teasing the hot knob and licking the knockers as they drooped over his face. For a while they both sucked on the shaft and glans, running their tongues over every inch of flesh, slipping the tongue under the knob, running it around and around, tickling the little pucker under the eye.

They were noisy lovers for they really slurped it up, moaning and gasping, smacking their lips and letting out all sorts of gasps as one could gulp down the whole shaft at once, squeals as they bit into the root of the other's wang and tugged at it trying to make it come loose, loud sucking and squishing noises as the cock would pop out of one mouth or the other. They were twitching all over the couch too.

First Dien was on top, and then Alan took over and thrust his hips with a vengeance, fucking Dien's mouth. Then they were on their sides and every variation of 69 imaginable. It was obvious that neither wanted to come right away for every so often one would yank his bursting dong out and rest for a moment. Their nuts became more swollen and each boy would suck first one nut and then the other. Both boys had really developed the retentive powers of their pricks. Their tongues laved the balls and then they began to rim each other. Alan particularly loved running his long thin tongue up a bung hole and then he licked all about Dien's tight brown pucker. Dien almost bucked Alan off the couch as his long pricklike tongue began to fuck in earnest. His squeals and sighs drew watchers closer to the exhibition and blow session. Alan let up for a moment.

"SUCK MY ASS...," he hissed, "DAMN YA. SHOVE IT IN...SHOVE...SHOVE! GOD...PLE...ASE!" This was new to Dien, but he was willing to try anything. So his fat tongue began to lick the cute pink pucker all over, about the entrance and into Alan's rectum. Both of them now rimmed and rimmed till the passionate onlookers could scarcely keep themselves out of the knot with the two boys. They could see the organ moving in the knockers, and suddenly each 69er latched onto the cock before his face, slipped into heaven and took it balls deep, and both asses tightened and bucked and twitched as two hot, heavy pungent discharges poured out of the two very heated pricks. The geysers of rod cream pleased both guys and they pumped for more and more, never gagging on the huge loads. This salty tang of love juice was a favorite diet of both of these handsome boys, and both squirmed lasciviously as though their very life's blood was oozing from them. The orgasms jerked spasmodically, exploding the last drops of come into the eager receiver.

Both boys did a clean-up job, licking and sucking every tasty drop off the other, and at last planted a loud juicy kiss on the end of the other's flaccid mass of drained sex. The iron-hard hammers had now dwindled to limp little rolls and slid out of the hot caverns, lolling along their sides, the boys now relaxed still in a 69 position but with their heads resting on tired bellies and a limp cock in their exhausted mouths as they continued to suck slowly.

The others wasted no time, so Kevin began. He was yet to blow his first cock, so he had buried his head between Robin's thighs as each relaxed on the cushioned floor. His own cock was again beating a regular tom-tom on his belly. Greg smeared the silver nectar spouting from his own rammer over the aching shaft and pointed the sturdy interloper at Kevin's bung hole— which still gaped open from the recent onslaught. He squirmed and wiggled as Greg shoved his curved cutlass to the root in this bounding ass. The impetuous intruder went right in the well-oiled passage and began its work.

Kevin was too occupied with licking, sucking, and kissing the lollypop in his mouth. This was the very first blow job he had ever initiated, and he was enjoying it...running his hands over the body of the manly, lewd, photographer as his lips sucked for dear life. His tongue fluttered over the bone-hard gristle and traced the swollen veins from the root to the tip of the shaft. Kevin pierced his tongue into the gaping slit and planted kiss after kiss on the shining crimson knob. Kevin's hands massaged Robin's groin and balls, but finally as his sucking became more violent and intense, he ran his fingers in the crease of Robin's rear and finally one or two fingers worked just as far as possible into Robin's hot, moist bung hole.

Kevin had the full shaft in his throat and he was biting into the base and the pubic hairs, when Robin began to squirm and thrust and buck his crotch into Kevin's face, and he began a regular fuck motion as he gasped and moaned and finally burst out, "OH GOD SUCK SUCK BITE IT SUCK HARDER IT'S COMING, IT'S COMING...AAAAAaasaa...Ooooohhhh...!"

He held himself rigid, his whole body vibrated and shook as he shot his load, the seminal fluids bursting down Kevin's burning throat. Kevin missed not one drop, swallowing volley after volley as it squirted into his mouth.

Kevin was too eager to stop; he extracted the softening blob and licked and kissed and sucked the last salty taste off. About now, Kevin realized he was being violated in two other directions. Greg was fucking with a vengeance. A guy would be crazy to pull out of paradise with nothing to lose but a wad. Kevin's ass was so very tight and rounded that Greg enjoyed thrusting hard into the firm rump and feeling his big thighs bounce back from the firm muscles of the buttocks.

Kevin had a deep tan, so his dark brown flanks looked as though he wore a tiny pair of white trunks. Greg was on his side pumping his hot cock into this beautiful ass. His own tail quivered and jerked as he wiggled about and twisted from side to side, pounding his big aching prick deeper and deeper into Kevin.

He reached around the hips, forgetting for a moment that Curt was busy on that front. His hands groped for Kevin's dong but hit Curt instead. A moan from the passionate cocksucker made him draw back, for Curt was licking and sucking the tremendous apparatus Kevin supported between his legs. The flat of his tongue was running up and down the shaft, and then the tip began to flutter around the glans until Kevin's squirms and moans showed that the passion was mounting and his load was about to erupt. The inner massage had really fired him. Curt was a noisy juicy blow artist. As his face was plugged with four to eight inches of thick dong, he moaned and groaned, and generally showed that he adored his hobby of milking hot eager pricks of cocky, eager, pretty boys.

"Suck harder, Curt!" encouraged Greg. "SEE IF YOU CAN GET A TASTE OF THIS!" Greg was ground to his balls in Kevin's ass, and his glans was quivering and twitching a volley of gism into the love grotto. Kevin gasped as his hips swayed to and fro, meeting Curt's mouth, sending his tool down his throat, releasing a flow of starchy syrup to take the place of the load that was being left in his behind.

Curt had clamped his teeth into the root of the stalk in his mouth and his throat muscles milked greedily. Kevin was squirming like mad as his discharge poured out at the same moment as Greg's. His body barely touched the floor mat as he tensed his muscles for the orgasm. To join in on the fun, Robin, who had recovered sufficiently to part the cheeks of Curt's cute ass, was running his tongue up and down the crease and into the tight bung hole that quivered from the tickling sensation.

Dien had curled up near Kevin's ass and as Greg's slick penis squished out of the hot hole, Dien took the jewels in his hand and licked and sucked all the juice off and stuffed most of the flaccid dauber and empty sack of balls into his mouth. When he was licked clean, Dien turned to the prostrate, exhausted body of Kevin and ran his tongue over the sweaty butt, his nose parted the handsome rear and his long, broad tongue liked his job of licking and washing from the crease of Kevin's ass the copious love juice.

This was the first time Kevin had ever been rimmed and he adored it. He just relaxed and purred as he spread his legs and arched his hips. His butt had experienced some rough treatment this past hour, and Dien's soft tongue soothed and quieted the twitching in his stretched cover.

Alan, too, was busy. His attention was turned to the prick of all pricks and his hands encircled Curt's long pulsing wang. He held tight to the shank and pumped his fists up and down playing him off, sliding the loose skin on his wang until it was bone-hard and throbbing. Alan continued to frig and jerk the monstrous mast in his hands, occasionally running the palm of one hand over its head, causing Curt's whole body to tense and squirm at the sensation. Alan was still fist-fucking Curt when the grand orgasm took place and he continued to pet and pump the lusty prodder. Curt was getting his kicks from all the caresses and squeezes his tool was getting. "LET'ER FLY, CURT!" and Alan chunked his fists hard into the groin a couple times.

The volcano erupted like a geyser, flying into the group, as

Curt went berserk with the rapturous sensation, to the accompaniment of screams from the watching boys. Little puddles landed everywhere and all the boys lapped up what they could find, as though they had never tasted Curt's spunk before.

CHAPTER EIGHT
THE GLORY HOLE

The "glory hole" is practically an institution in the realm of unmitigated sexual release. There is nothing so impersonal, so calculated, so absolutely void of personality as the glory hole. Like the erotic short story, it represents pure, unadulterated sex. Its sole purpose is sex and there are no embellishments, no romance, no overtures connected with it. The hole permits exposure of the male genitals and nothing more. The body, face, hands, etc., are completely obliterated. The penis is surrounded by a blank wall and all that is concentrated upon is the sense of touch.

The atmosphere of the public restroom holds a mysterious fascination for certain individuals. This is indeed unfortunate because public restrooms have proven to be the downfall of many homosexuals. Our laws are strict with regard to public indecency, and the overt homosexual would be wise to refrain from frequenting such places when searching for sexual excitement.

The following story is really not too far-fetched. It is a realistic account of what oft-times happens in the public restroom of a local theater on a quiet afternoon.

* * * * * *

I suppose that if it had not been such a hot afternoon (summer in Phoenix can be real hell), and had I not had my appointments canceled at the last minute, I might have never gotten bored enough to take in a movie.

I was a stranger in the city, however, and there was just nothing else to do. I figured a double feature of something would be better than going back to my motel. I was attending a sales convention and there was no escape from the group. I picked a movie house that was showing an old Joan Crawford film that I had missed the first ten times around. It was on a side street and off the beaten path. I wanted to be sure that no one from my company would just happen to wander in and we'd suddenly be stuck with each other's company for the balance of the afternoon.

I got my ticket and went in about ten minutes before the feature that was on was scheduled to break. It was enough time for a cigarette, so I went to the john for a smoke. I wasn't above cruising johns, but I had always heard that Phoenix was a pretty dead place, and what I had seen in the four days I had been there had convinced me my informants were right. Just as I suspected, the john was dirty and deserted.

I whipped out my cock and took a leak while I read the writing over the urinal. SHOW IT HARD FOR BLOW. SLAVE WHO LOOKS LIKE MASTER-WANTS MASTER! There were three urinals in a row and at the end of the row were two wooden stalls. I could see the peep hole carved through, but no eye was peeking out at my emptying dick. I gave the old cock a flip and tucked it back in my shorts. Just the acrid smell of the place and the scribbled notes had given me a little bit of a hard-on. I thought of how nice it would be to have a warm mouth to bury it in.

I walked over and pushed the door on the first of the two stalls open and went in. I decided that I would wait and see what intermission brought to the pissers. There might be a nice-looking dick or two in the audience—if there was anybody in the audience at all.

Opposite the peephole that looked out on the urinals, there was a glory hole. It was large for a glory hole for even big dicks.

It looked more like an open oven door. At least it would give you not only a look at your visitor's equipment, but a good look at him (or her, as the case may be.)

There were a couple of stories on the wall. One about some guy who had picked up a cowboy and had taken him home to fuck his wife and how they had fucked her both at the same time, and then how the cowboy had fucked the guy while his wife blew him. Naturally, the cowboy was made out to be a Greek god with a cock down to his knees. There were a couple of darn good illustrations at the side of the story of good luck, probably drawn by someone who had read the story at a later date. The pale green wall was stained all around the story with a helluva lot of wasted come. I can't say that it didn't affect me too, for my cock was fully hard now and throbbing for a little attention. I dropped a couple of beads of spit on the head to keep it nice and moist and to make it feel just a little bit better when I rubbed my hand back and forth over the head.

The movie broke just about then, or so I would guess, because the door popped open and in came a half dozen men. I glued my eye discreetly to the peephole, but the guy in the first stall stood too close and I didn't get to see anything for quite a while. He really must of had to piss.

Finally, he stepped away and I got to see at least a half dozen cocks before the supply petered out. There were a couple of interesting ones: one in particular that snagged my attention. It wasn't very long apparently, but had a head on it like a door-knob. It was sort of dark brown, so I figured it belonged to one of the many Indians around the place. He kept slipping the fore-skin back and forth over the head until it was all shiny. When he pissed it came out in a flat stream about an inch wide. I would have liked to see the hole in that head. There was a moder-ately big one on some young fellow in a sport jacket, but he conducted himself and his dick in a most business-like manner, so I assumed he didn't go that route.

Everybody had finally cleared out of the john and I was just getting up and putting my now fully disturbed cock back into my jockeys when the door popped open again and another guy came in. He walked directly to the stall next to mine and came in. I quickly sat down, just in case it might prove interesting.

When I saw him I was tempted to get back up and go. He certainly wasn't very attractive. He had a bushy head of black hair and a flat nose. He looked like he had just come in from the reservation. Short and heavy-built too. Kind of an interesting square and stocky body, if it hadn't been for the face.

Just as I was getting ready to move, he dropped his pants and turned to me. That boy didn't have to be attractive with what he had hanging there. Six big fat limp inches hung out from between the hair in his crotch. He stood there just long enough for me to get a good look, then he plunked his ass down on the toilet seat. I expected to hear a splash as his big uncircumcised cock flopped into the water. We sat there for a while doing nothing. I could only see him about half way up his chest through the hole, and all of his legs and waist were visible looking down through the hole. He had unbuttoned his light shirt and the muscles on his stomach looked like a scrub board; solid and firm.

He sat with both his hands in his crotch so that I could see nothing. Not a muscle anywhere on him twitched. I watched and began to discreetly play with myself. I had the feeling he was watching, but he was leaning far enough back that I could not be sure without actually looking up at him through the hole. Little by little I let more and more of my cock show. I wasn't exactly ashamed of the piece of meat I had. It had been called big by some and adequate by most. It was exactly eight and one half inches long and no cheating when it was measured, straight as an arrow and big enough around that you couldn't get your hand closed around it anywhere.

I showed it to my friend next door and noticed that though he didn't move much, he moved his hands in his crotch a little and I could detect a steady motion or massaging taking place there. That was all the encouragement I needed. I stood up and let him see it sticking straight out from me. I guess I figured he would be carried away enough to stick his hand right through the hole and grab it. I guess you can't figure Indians like you figure most people. He didn't move a muscle and finally I sat back down. We sat there again for a moment, and then it was his turn. He stood up and in a single motion turned and stuck his now rock hard cock through the hole into my side of the booth.

God! What a magnificent tool that was. It was at least ten inches long and thicker than I imagined a cock could be. I wrapped my right hand around it and there was a gap of at least one half inch between my thumb and my finger. His throbbing piece of missile was a light brown color with a glistening pink head the size of a doorknob.

Doorknob! Then I realized suddenly that it was the same one that had caught my attention earlier. I guess when they are soft they seem darker then when they are hard. He kept pushing it toward me like he was fucking the air.

I had originally planned to have my cock sucked, but I wasn't about to argue with a piece of meat as big and nice as that. I managed to take the head in my mouth by opening my jaws just as far as they could go. The first time I had the head all the way in, I ran my tongue into the hole in the head. It was as big as I thought and I could get the whole tip of my tongue into it. That was the first one that I had ever had like that.

He started to grind his hips in a steady motion and rammed as much of his cock down my hot throat as he could. This wasn't much, for there was an awful lot left over when he was in me as far as he could get. I let him grind away for a while, and I rubbed my hand up over his stomach. Good solid iron. I reached down under his cock and hefted the balls in my hand. They weren't very big, but they hung low in their sac. As quickly as he had put his cock through the hole, he pulled it back and sat down.

"Let me swing on yours," he whispered. I got up all too willingly and shoved it at him. I watched that big mouth of his slide over the head of my cock and down that pulsing eight inch shaft again and again until, each time, his lips had buried themselves in my pubic hair and I could feel my cock prodding against the back of his throat.

I felt his hand under my balls and then they slowly began to work their way around the crack of my ass until they found the hole. Little by little he stuck his finger into me until between his sucking on my cock and fingering my ass I was trying to crawl up the partition. Just as he had me on the verge of pumping my load into him, he stopped and stood up and put his dick through the hole too. There we were with our dicks pressed against one another. He put his dick under mine so that it ran down into my balls when he pumped forward. Mine, of course, banged into his stomach at the end of the run. He wrapped both his hands around our cocks and then started to grind away again like it was the best fuck in the world.

After a little while we both had had enough of that. It had felt good though to have the head of his dick buried rhythmically in my balls. I dropped back to the seat and took that big thing in my mouth again and started to suck him like I had never sucked anyone before. I ran it as far back in my throat as I could get it and then I pulled it out as far as it could go without actually leaving my lips and licked it under the head where it was tenderest.

In no time at all I had that Indian ready for a war dance. He wanted to pull back again, but this time I didn't let him. I hung on to that huge pulsating staff of life and sucked and sucked until I felt him begin to tremble and to mumble something as his fucking my face became faster and faster. Then with a scream I am sure was heard all over the theater he bust his guts inside my hot lips. Cum streamed into me like water flowing from a faucet. It choked me and gushed out of my mouth like glowing hot lava, but I hung on and swallowed all that I could. It was trickling down my chin and down the wall of the booth onto the floor. His dick immediately started to get smaller and smaller and I kept sucking it until I was sure he was dry. That was one well-spent buck, I hope to tell you.

He rested for a moment and then he got up so quickly and pulled up his pants and was gone that I didn't realize what he was doing. He either had some sort of Freudian recriminations afterward or was just the bashful type. At any rate, there I was alone with a roaring hard-on, ready to explode at the slightest touch.

I wasn't about to go out and watch Joan Crawford try to repel some man who I'd flip to get at, so I just sat there and started to read some of the other "literature" on the walls. I hated to waste the good load I had built up by jacking off, and so I sat hoping that someone would come in the other stall who would be interested in my constantly enlarging love organ. Luckily I didn't have too long to wait.

This one was just a kid, about eighteen or nineteen, I'd guess. Kind of scrawny, but in that young rangy athletic way that so many kids his age are. At that point, I wouldn't have cared if he were only thirteen. I wanted to get that cock of mine in some guy's mouth and blow a hole out the back of his head with my load.

We played the usual cat and mouse game for a few minutes. He kept his pants drawn up over his knees so that I couldn't see anything except his hand shoved down in between his crotch playing with himself. I knew he was watching me, so I just pulled my dick out into plain view and gave it a few healthy whacks that brought a couple drops of ooze to the crack in the head. Apparently this was all the encouragement the kid needed, for he put his hand up to the hole and motioned for me to stick my dick through. I didn't waste any time in complying with his wishes.

At first he just started to lick it all over with his tongue. I could watch him by leaning backward. His tongue darted all over that big cock of mine covering it with enough spit and slime to slide it through the eye of a needle. He was just about driving me mad and I guess he could tell from the way that my dick kept jerking up and down. He tongued down my dick to my balls and swallowed each of those for a couple of minutes, all the while sliding his hand back and forth over my rod. I felt like I was on fire with his hot tongue all over me and hand sliding on my tool. I couldn't take it any longer, and afraid that I would pop in the air and waste it all, I jerked it back through the hole.

The kid seemed to sense what the problem was and when he put his open lips next to the hole I pushed the cock into his mouth like I was going to nail him to the opposite wall. I could feel it push by his tonsils and sink deep down into his throat. The little bastard didn't even gag. I wasn't the first cock that had fucked him in the face.

And fuck him in the face is just what I did. I put my hands through the hole and grabbed his face with them and held him right up against the wall while I pulled my dick out of him and rammed it down his throat again and again, each time getting a little faster. The kid had his hand through the hole and was hanging on to my balls, trying to run his finger up the crack of my ass. It drove me off my rocker for a little while, and I guess I lost control, because I really started to slam that cock to him.

I could tell I was beginning to get to him, because he kept trying to pull his head away and I just held him by the ears so that he couldn't move and pounded my dick into his tonsils again and again. When I fired my load, I thought I was going to have my guts come out with it. My whole insides seemed to drop when I came, and there was a sensation of suddenly flying and seeing all sorts of whirling stars. Cum was gushing out everywhere and I could hear the kid gasping and choking and trying to swallow so that he could breath.

I quickly let go of his ears. He pulled his head back and gave a couple of quick pants and grunts, but never stopped licking the head of my tender tool until it was too limp to stand. I fell exhausted back against the other wall and then sat down on the toilet seat and tried to get hold of myself again. In a few minutes the world was in its proper perspective.

I had sat for a couple of minutes longer and was just about to get up and pull up my pants and see how Miss Crawford was doing, when the kid shoved his hand through the hole. There was a picture in his hand and my curiosity was great enough to take it and look at it. It was the picture of a very small boy, probably about sixteen and about five feet six inches tall, being screwed by another young fellow in his twenties. The picture was a good close up and showed the huge hunk of meat that the older boy had.

Looking at it for a minute, I could just see the asshole of the sixteen-year-old stretching trying to accommodate the instrument that was tearing it. I handed it back to the kid and he shoved another one through to me. This one showed another guy on his back (you couldn't see his face because he had his legs up in the air and arched back) and there was another middle-aged man with just the head of his dick in the other guy's ass. Needless to say, it was a pretty big dick. The third picture the kid showed me was of the two fellows in the first picture. The sixteen-year-old was sitting on the older boy's lap, the cock buried all the way up his shit-shoot, and the older kid was sucking on the younger's cock.

By the time I had handed the last of the pictures back to my "buddy" next door, I was all upset and hard again. Apparently this is what had been the purpose of the pictures for the kid stood up and let me get my first look at his meat. If the pictures hadn't aroused me, his cock sure would have. It was just a little longer than mine, probably nine inches, and straight as an arrow with a sort of heart-shaped head. It looked nice and thick and right then and there I decided to go for broke and see if I could make the twice in a row bit. The kid was reluctant apparently to put it through the hole so I could get at it and when I stuck mine through the hole he just gave it a friendly pat. I pulled back when he whispered, "Turn around."

Suddenly I got the picture. I had been fucked before, but never in a standing position and never quite in "public"...and *dry*. Spit, I felt, wasn't going to accommodate that delicious morsel of man. However, never one to be a party pooper, I turned my ass to the hole and hesitantly backed up. I expected to feel that shaft trying to force its way into me. I was totally unprepared for what happened. Suddenly, there was his long warm tongue licking up the crack in my ass. His hands spread the cheeks and he started to drive his tongue up inside of me. The warm moist feeling soon had me pushing my ass back at him so he could get deeper in me. At the same time I was wiggling my hips and fucking the air in front of me.

Good? You don't know unless you have tried it. He kept up his licking and tonguing until he knew he had me hot enough for just about anything, and then I felt something cold slide in my ass on his finger. He came prepared with Vaseline. At least it would make it a little easier, because I was determined to get that cock of his in me if I had to sit on it with only spit to help.

Gently his hands pulled the cheeks apart as far as they would go and I felt him place the head of his tool right at the hole. Little by little he began to work that thing inside of me. The first push he gave to break the barrier put all of the big heart-shaped head in me and just about finished me off. I knew then that that dick looked only half the size it was. With the head in me he started his drive home.

It was slow at first. He worked an inch or so into me with each gentle stroke until I could feel him pounding that meat well up into the gut of me. I figured that I had it all, but each stroke seemed to drive it just a little big deeper. I knew I couldn't take much more, and gave a little quiet sigh when I finally felt his balls come to rest on my ass. I guess I sighed too soon, for then he began to fuck me. I had to brace my shoulders and back against the opposite wall to keep from coming apart with his lunges.

He slammed that thing into me like I had no bottom. I gave a cry the first time he did, but it didn't stop him or even make him hesitate. He had hold of my balls and had pulled them back between my legs, hanging on tight, so there was no place I could go and nothing I could do but let him have his way and slam his meat into me as hard as he wanted.

It was only bad for the first couple of minutes and then he had opened the nine or ten inch channel that he needed, and everything began to feel better as my ass stretched to accept his swollen piece of passion.

Man, that kid knew how to fuck. He'd pull it all the way out until my ass would almost snap shut on the head, and then he'd drive it into me with every ounce of strength he had. Little by little, I began to work with him (even if it did hurt sometimes when he reached bottom the wrong way) and he let go of my balls. Then he started a cork screw motion that really had me hanging on.

Faster and faster his pumping became and I could tell from the way his heavy balls slapped against the crack of my ass that he was going to shoot his wad. In a thrust that drove deeper into me than any of the others, he let me have it. Cum burnt up inside of me like white hot coal and I jumped at the heat of the discharge and the force with which it shot into me. He held his dick in me until it started to get soft and then I felt the bastard start to piss in me.

I tried to pull away (I don't go for that shit—yet!) but he had me by the balls again and there was nothing I could do. Finally, when he pulled out, piss and cum shot all over the place as I tried to get my ass on the stool. I'm glad that there was just the two of us in the place, because the piss and the air coming out of me must have sounded like hell. I was relieved to see that there was no blood, so I guess the fucking hadn't been too bad. The way my insides and cock burned and twitched though, I knew I was hot as all hell again.

As the last fart exploded, the kid handed me a note, written on toilet paper in pencil. *That was Great Man. I Got a Buddy Outside Who'd Like some of That. He's Got a Big One.*

Interested? I read the note again and then sort of shrugged my shoulders. His next note asked *what's wrong?* I penciled a reply to that one. *I want to get my nuts off too.* His answer: *My buddy will take care of that too. He's Great.* Why not, I said to myself, and so I nodded when his face appeared at the hole. He dressed and left and I whipped the last of the moisture off my ass and wondered what the next one was going to be like. I couldn't last much longer and had to get back to the motel or there would be a lot of explaining to do.

I didn't quite expect what his buddy was going to be like, and was more than a little bit surprised. The blackest, tallest, skinniest Negro I have never seen walked into the stall, dropped his pants and sat down. I still had my mouth open from surprise when another piece of toilet tissue came through the hole. *My name's Pat. My buddy says that you got a sweet ass.* I crumpled the paper and dropped it into the john.

I was still debating what to do; whether to get up and leave or to make the best of it, when the guy got up and dropped his limp dick through the hole. I can honestly say that I have never seen one bigger than that. It was dead soft and it hung a good eight or nine inches down the wall.

I just sort of gasped, and if there had been any question before, there was certainly no question now. There is a little of the size queen in all of us and I knew right when I saw it that I was going to have it. Coal-black or not! I ran my hand up along it and skinned it back and watched the big purple-black head slip out of the foreskin. Even in the dull light of the john it glistened.

As I played with it, it started to get harder and longer, and longer and longer until it stood staring me right in the eye. It was a foot long, twelve thick black juicy inches long, or it wasn't an inch. "Suck me, baby, suck me," he whispered, and I leaned forward to oblige. I put my lips around that black tool and swung on it like it was the sweetest thing in the world, and right then, it was. I wrapped my right hand around the base and held it while I pushed as much in my throat as I could. All the while I was sucking on the huge piece of male ebony, I could hear him softly whispering, "Suck me, baby, eat that big black motherfucker, let me feel your lips drain me, man." Just listening to him made me hot enough to pop, but the combination of his soft murmuring voice and the slow, but steady, pumping of his hips made me want to get as much of that buck into me as possible. I wanted to be fucked by him and I knew that was what he wanted too.

Abruptly I stood up and shoved my ass up against that big

black tool and braced myself for him to push it into me. Instead, like his buddy, he rimmed me first. Only this time, I really got rimmed. His tongue must have been as long as his dick, for once he got started I know I had four or five inches of thick pink-black tongue whipping around inside my ass. One thing, it was clean since it had just been flushed out. When he got me good and hot, I couldn't wait any longer. "Fuck, me," I said.

As I looked over my shoulder, I saw him rubbing Vaseline on it. God! How it glistened, black and unbelievably long! The glory hole was just big enough for him to get his hand through and he reached through and grabbed me by the waist and pulled me back toward him. With one long steady push he shoved his way into me.

The pain was unbelievable and I began to struggle and it was all I could do not to yell, but his determination was absolute and his grip was like a steel vise. His finger marks left black and blue spots on my skin for about a week after that. He just kept pushing and pushing and forcing more and more into me until he had to stop because there was no place left to put it. My insides were burning like fire, but there was no stopping me, or him. I couldn't stop because he had control and he wasn't for losing control. He began to screw me like he was possessed by something. He'd take long grinding strokes that would pull that big black tower all the way out of me and then slam it back in with all the strength of a steel rod.

My asshole was snapping closed and open so many times that it began to really ache. Each time he drove into me he went a little further than the time before, and the pain made me want to get away, but I couldn't. I couldn't feel his balls against me yet, so I knew that I didn't have it all in me. After a couple of long fast strokes he pulled it all the way out and then he started just to fuck me with the head. He'd pull it out until my asshole closed and then he'd ease it back in and sort of whirl it around a few times and then pull it all the way out again.

The pain of a few strokes earlier was quickly forgotten in this rhythm and I began to tense and relax to his strokes. The pleasure of that big black head rubbing around just inside my guts was unbelievable. With one of his big hands he let go of my hips and reaching around in front of me he started to play with my cock which was standing at rigid attention. I reached down under my legs and felt his slippery dick as it kept sliding in and out of my ass. It was real crazy feeling that big thing slip over my fingers and into the opening in me, and it excited me enough to back up against him again. He dropped my dick and grabbed my waist again.

This time he really started to screw me. He wasn't fooling around, and judging from his panting I knew that the time was getting awful close that something was going to happen. Apparently he had been considerate before, for when he lunged into me this time he really went all out. I felt something give in me that had never been touched before, and though the pain was quick and intense, I felt his balls come to rest in the crack of my ass and I knew that I had that twelve inch piece of black African meat buried right up to the hilt in my white ass.

I was so hot now that I didn't care what was happening inside. I wanted to feel him explode his load in me and I wanted to shoot mine anywhere. The pain in my balls was beginning to be overwhelming. He was working away with a frenzy now and he drove in further and further and harder and harder. I could feel that marvelous wonderful piece of cock getting bigger and bigger in me.

With one terrific movement he pulled the whole damn thing out of me, and then slammed it back into me, and all the way up until his balls slapped my ass. He came. Right then and there he shot that power pack of hot white cum into me. I could just close my eyes and picture that big purple-black head spitting its hot load of white cream into my guts. I grabbed my meat and started to beat it like hell and in a second I shot a wad clear across the booth and splattered it all over the other wall.

We just hung there like that for a few minutes. Both of us were too limp and too exhausted to move. Gradually he began to pull that black dick of his out of me and I could feel it slide inch by inch down and out of me. I let it go with a big pop and sank exhausted onto the stool. Man, that was the greatest.

I had a little trouble with my ass after that fucking, but my doctor fixed it up and after a couple of months I was back in practice again. Every time I go back to Phoenix, I stop at this little theater. The glory hole is still there, and when I see a little trail of dried blood on the wall, I know that my black friend has just gotten to somebody else. Next time I see him, I'll be ready.

CHAPTER NINE
DEAR BUDDY

This tale utilizes a style-device common in nearly every level of erotica, from classical works to the lowest form of hard core pornography—the personal letter. In some variations, this becomes a diary or journal, such as with *My Secret Life,* or *Fanny Hill,* but frequently it remains a letter, as it is here.

Also, *Dear Buddy* brings us again to the man in uniform, this time a handsome Marine. Strangely, it is the Marine and the Sailor who are most frequently described in these stories. The U.S. Army fares somewhat better, and rarely does one read of the Air Force. Similarly, a study dating back some years found that graffiti in military installations varied with the branch of the service—Naval and Marine installations tended toward homosexual graffiti to a high degree, the Army toward hetero-sexual graffiti, and the Air Force toward an absence of graffiti altogether.

* * * * * * *

Dear Buddy,

Most of the guys have gone down to the PX for a beer, but I thought I'd stay here and write you instead. We've been having rifle practice all week, and I'm pretty tired tonight. Being a Marine is sure a lot of work!

Something happened last week-end that I thought you might

like to know about. I got a pass last Friday night so I hitch-hiked up to L.A. I was lucky and got a ride all the way with a guy named Jerry. He was young and nice-looking and very friendly, and after we drove a while, he stopped and bought me dinner and a few drinks afterward. That made me feel real good! Then we drove up some hills and stopped to look at the view. It was plenty dark, and we talked a lot, and I told him all about the farm and everything back home. He was plenty surprised when I told him I was only nineteen, but he said I looked real athletic and that was probably what fooled him.

Then he slid over next to me and put his hand on my leg. That felt real funny and I didn't know quite what to do, but he kept running his fingers up and down my thigh and pretty soon my pecker started acting up and getting hard. I hoped he wouldn't notice, but I guess he could feel it right through my pants, and he just laughed and told me to relax.

Then he opened my fly and reached inside to play around, and finally he pulled my cock and balls out where he could get to them easier. By this time my rod was awful hard and he started rubbing it the way you and I used to do out in the barn. He kept saying how fine it was, although I didn't know there was any other kind, and finally he bent over and kissed the top of it. Then he kissed me right on the mouth, and I could feel his tongue running over my lips.

I'd never been kissed like that before, and I didn't know what to do, but he just grinned and said he'd teach me about it later. He went on playing with my dick and saying how beautiful and big it was, and then he started kissing it and licking it again. He told me that it wasn't easy to take care of one that was so long and had such a big knob on the end of it, but he wanted to have it.

Then he licked it some more, and when it was dripping wet, he started sucking it right into his mouth. I guess it must have gone right down his throat because pretty soon he had all of it. I just sat there and watched it slide in and out between his lips, and it really felt good! He got his hands up under my shirt and rubbed them all over me, and then he played with my nuts while he went right on sucking on my pole. I thought I'd go nuts, and finally I couldn't stand it anymore and I shot my wad, and he swallowed every bit of it. Criminie, that sure felt good!

Well, I hoped he'd do that again, but after we'd rested awhile, Jerry put my gear back inside my shorts and fastened my pants. Then we drove into town and up to his place for a drink. It was a very nice place, and Jerry told me I could stay overnight because he didn't think I could get a room so late.

We finished a couple of drinks, and then he told me to go in and take a shower while he made some more. He had a real fancy bathroom with a big tub and a separate shower and a rug on the floor and everything, and I took my time undressing while I looked at everything. I'd just gotten into the shower when Jerry came in and jumped in with me. I'd showered with other guys around in the Marines and back home in the high school gym, but that was nothing like this!

He was blond and tanned and had a pretty good build, and he kept staring at me and saying how nice I looked without any clothes on. We horsed around until we were both wet all over, and then we took turns covering each other with soap lather. It really felt good to stand there with the warm water spraying against my back and Jerry spreading soap suds all over me and playing with my dong.

I was surprised at how nice it felt to rub my hands over Jerry's shoulders and chest, and when I got down to his belly, he laughed and grabbed my wrists and shoved my fingers right into his crotch. His pecker stood straight out and felt warm and strong, and his balls hung down loose and slippery. He didn't like me to play with his nuts because he said I was too rough, and he had me turn around and rinse off while he scrubbed my back. It really felt strange when he rubbed his hands over my butt and slid his fingers right between my cheeks, and he laughed at the way I tightened up when he touched my asshole.

Then he got under the shower while I washed his back, and I shoved a whole handful of lather between his cheeks. He just chuckled and leaned back so his butt was right against my dick, and I thought for a minute I was going to come just from the way that felt. He made me cool off under the shower, and then we dried off and went into the bedroom and laid down on the bed while we had the drinks Jerry had fixed earlier. He kept running his hands over my chest and down between my legs and everywhere, and my pecker stood straight up the whole time.

Well, buddy, by this time I felt pretty cozy! I'd had an awful lot to drink, and what with Jerry fooling around and all, about the only thing I could think about was having my rod shoot again. Jerry pushed me back on the bed and started kissing me all over—my nipples and armpits and balls and the tip of my cock and everywhere.

Then he kissed me on the lips again, and this time he jammed his tongue right into my mouth. Gees, that was good, and I kissed him back the same way! My dong was beginning to drip by this time, and he slid down between my legs and started sucking it hard. It felt real wild, and the next thing I knew, I was holding his head down and shoving my cock into his throat while it fired like a cannon. When it was all over, he stretched out flat on top of me, holding his prick against my belly and squirming around until he shot his juice all over me. Then we rested for a while, and then he wiped his cream off me with a towel and we got under the covers and went to sleep.

Sleeping with a naked guy next to you is really very nice, buddy. I guess Jerry was used to it because he slept like a log, but I kept waking up and fooling around with him. It was a lot of fun to touch him all over, and once I wanted to see what his dick was like when he was asleep, so I played with it a little. It was hard to believe that flabby little thing could get so hard, so I slid down to see what it was like to lick it. It tasted kind of funny, but I didn't mind it, and finally I tried sucking it the way he'd sucked mine. I didn't think I'd like that much, but it was sort of fun, especially when it got hard. I was sure surprised that he didn't wake up!

Jerry brought me breakfast in bed the next morning and was

very nice to me and told me I could stay all week-end. It was a fine day, and we decided to go to the beach. I didn't have any trunks, but Jerry knew about a place where it wouldn't make any difference, so we went there. We had the place all to ourselves so we took off all our clothes and went swimming and lay around sleeping and drinking beer. Jerry had brought his camera, and he took a lot of pictures of me. We had a real good time, and I got a swell tan.

Jerry had invited some friends over for cocktails that evening, and I was just getting ready to shower when they came in. I was stripped to my shorts, but Jerry insisted I come out and have a drink with them. One of them was named Jack, and I liked him a lot. He was a couple of years older than me and quite handsome and rugged-looking. He had also been in the Marines, so we had a lot to talk about.

The other man was named Bob, and he and Jerry seemed to be very fond of each other because they kissed several times. After several drinks, Jerry began to tell them how we had met, and I felt kind of embarrassed when he started describing how I was hung and all. He said my knob was bigger than most guys' whole dick, but I didn't really believe him. Finally Jack and Jerry went out to the kitchen to make some more drinks, and Bob came over to where I stood and started feeling around in the crotch of my shorts.

Then he pulled my shorts down and was playing with my balls when the others came back. They all laughed, and then Jerry told me to go and take my shower. I had started the water going and was just about to get in when Jack came in with another drink. We talked and drank a little, and then he suggested that he wash my back in the shower.

I finished my drink while he began to undress, and I couldn't keep from staring at him. He was very tan and a lot more muscular than Jerry, and his chest was covered with black hair that grew on down over his stomach in a thin line. I felt kind of nervous when he started to unfasten his pants, so I jumped into the shower, and a couple of minutes later, he got in behind me and started washing my back.

When he had me covered with lather, he put his arms around me and pressed against me while he rubbed the soap bar over my chest and stomach and played with my cock. Then he turned me around and grabbed me and kissed me. It was a long, wonderful kiss, and I thought for a moment that I would go off all over him.

Then he pulled back and I reached down for his dick. It was stiff as a rod and a lot thicker and longer than Jerry's, and I really liked playing with it a lot. Finally he took my pole and put it right beside his so I could handle both of them at once, and they were just about exactly the same size. His balls were pretty big too, and he got real excited when I fooled with them. It was kind of like what you and I used to do except that we never did it in the shower.

Well, we finally finished showering and dried off, and then Jack took me into the bedroom and we lay down on the bed together. I really like the way Jack held me real tight and rubbed his chest hair against me, and we kissed an awful lot.

Then we wrestled a little, and I got plenty excited because he seemed to know a lot of tricks to make me feel good. He crawled all over me, and my heart got to pounding so hard I could hardly breathe.

Finally he had me lay back while he got down between my legs and kissed my nuts and licked my cock good. Suddenly he got up on his hands and knees over me and bent forward so his love-muscle was coming right down toward my mouth. I wanted to show him that I knew what to do, so I reached up and grabbed it and steered it to my lips. I started licking it, and the knob was real big and smooth like an egg, and it wasn't long before it was slipping into my mouth.

Jack sat back on his haunches and pulled me up by the shoulders so I could bend over and take it easier. I worked on it pretty hard, and soon he was groaning and his whole body was shaking with excitement. Gees, it was wild! Suddenly his dong began to jerk and he jammed it all the way into my throat, and then I was gulping down the hot cream that was shooting from it. I kept swallowing and swallowing until it finally stopped coming, and then he twisted around right away and got his lips around my dripping tool. I sure gave him a mouthful of juice!

Jack and I rested a little and then we went into the living room again. Jerry and Bob were lying naked on the floor, and their peters were real soft and limp. I was kind of surprised that they weren't nearly as big as Jack and mine. Well, Jerry fixed a light supper, and we sat around in the dark and ate and went right on drinking.

I got pretty high, and I guess the other guys did too. Jack and I got to fooling around, and the next thing I knew, Bob was on the floor on his back with Jerry on his hands and knees over him facing the other direction and they were sucking each other at the same time. I felt kind of funny watching them, and when Jack touched my cock, it stood up nice and straight.

He went into the bathroom for a minute, and when he came back, he had a jar of Vaseline in his hand. The next thing I knew he was spreading grease all over my pecker, and then he had me get down on my knees behind Jerry. He pushed some more Vaseline right into Jerry's ass, and then he took my tool and shoved it into Jerry's crack. I felt the head of my rod push against Jerry's asshole, and he started twisting around like maybe it hurt a little.

Jack said to go ahead and jam it in, and when I did, my flange slipped right into his hole. That really felt fine! Jerry kept right on sucking Bob, and as I started pumping my pole in and out of him, Jack began rubbing his hands over my butt. He finally got his finger right in between my cheeks, and every time I'd shove my dick into Jerry, Jack would push his finger against my hole. Well, this all got me pretty worked up so it didn't hardly hurt at all when Jack's finger got all the way into me. I could hear Jerry making some pretty wild sounds, but I couldn't stop, and I kept pumping my cock in and out of his hole until it finally fired another load of that fine juice.

I certainly felt fine, and while I was in the bathroom cleaning up, Jerry came in and said that Jack was so excited he was "browning" Bob. I surely would have liked to see that. Jerry said that he liked the way I had fucked him and he hoped I'd do it again sometime, and I said I would be glad to.

Well, after we got cleaned up, we had some more drinks, and then Jerry fixed up the couch for Jack and me to sleep on while he and Bob took the bedroom. When we got into bed, Jack put his arms around me and held me very close while he kissed me over and over. It felt awfully good, and I guess we both enjoyed it a lot. He was quite rugged and well-built, but he was also very nice, and he promised to teach me a lot of things if I'd spend a week-end with him. Finally he rolled me over on my side away from him and put his cock between my thighs. I really liked having him next to me that way with his arms around me and his crotch hairs rubbing against my butt! All night long he kept waking me up so we could suck each other whenever we got hard.

I was kind of tired the next day, so Jack and I went to the beach and in the evening he drove me all the way back to the base. Just before we got there, he pulled off the road so we could suck each other one more time. That's really a lot of fun, and Jack says I'm getting to be quite good at it. He promised to pick me up here next Friday so we can go to his place for the week-end. I think that will be a lot of fun.

Well, that's what happened last week-end, Buddy. I sure didn't know there were guys like Jerry and Bob and Jack, but now I'm real glad I met them. Maybe the next time I get home on leave I can show you some of the things they've shown me. I know you'll like it as much as I do.

I guess I better sign off for this time. The rest of the guys aren't back from the PX yet, but that nice young platoon sergeant I told you about last time just came in and said he'd be glad to wash my back if I wanted to take a shower. It was awful nice of him to offer and I sure could use a shower, so I think I'll go along with him.

Your Buddy

CHAPTER TEN
SEXPERIENCES

Sexperiences is not so much a story as what seems to be an authentic account of the narrator's particular sexual experiences, many of which are indeed a bit unusual. As such, it represents an excellent case history for serious study; the author has avoided the customary exaggeration, describing modest organs and only boasting slightly in regard to the number of orgasms he has been able to achieve in one night, five being his record. Most of his activities center about masturbation, which he frankly admits is his favorite form of gratification. However, his experience is bisexual and includes many other forms of sexuality. One of the more unusual involves a sort of no-hands masturbation in the shower. Also of interest are the incestuous episodes with the subject's brother, and his desire for his father.

Yet for its peculiarities, *Sexperience* is not so out of place in this collection as it might at first seem. For in fact, all of these stories are personal accounts—either of actual experiences, slightly exaggerated, or of fantasy cravings. The authors of *Abdullah, I'll be a Horse's Ass*, and the other erotic stories in this book were motivated in much the same way as the author of *Sexperience*—and with much the same results.

* * * * * * *

Among my earliest recollections of sex experiences are those from the time when I was between three and four years old. It was then that I discovered the pleasurable sensation that developed when I held the foreskin of my little cock and twisted it between my fingers. I had great fun doing this for a while till I found out that the foreskin would pull back, and by working my hand up and down, the final sensation was even better. One day I was surprised to find that if I put my left hand in between my legs, I could get the end of my middle finger into my asshole. This was a wonderful discovery, and I played with myself in that way for several years. All this time I didn't realize that the other boys were probably doing it too. I don't remember when I found out that if another fellow did his jacking off at the same time, it made my own feel better.

My brother and I had a tree house with two stories which became a sort of club, and in the summer when the maple leaves were out in full, it made a fine place for privacy. There, many times, I played finger with myself—up the ass, and jerked off two or three times a day. In the summer we put mattresses up there and my brother and a friend slept on the top floor, while I, with one of my friends, slept on the lower tier. I think it was during this time that the fun of jerking off together developed. I remember what fun it was for both of us to get hard-ons and one pretend to be a doctor and crouch down to give a thorough examination to the other's parts. There was never any effort made to kiss or to touch the other fellows' prick except with the hands, and there is no recollection that at that time we ever tried to fuck the other up the ass. It was still fun to just jack off and if you did it while examining the other fellow's cock, it was more fun.

While I was alone I tried to find new ways of making it feel good. I was never circumcised and had quite a bit of foreskin. If I pulled the foreskin up over the head of the cock with the left hand, I could push my right middle finger down into the skin until it touched the head, and worked the skin up and down till I got the sensation. I called it "fucking myself."

One day when the family was away and my brother and I were alone at home, I happened to walk into our bedroom when he had his pants down and was jerking himself. He came over to me and took my prick out of my pants and jerked us both at the same time. He must have been scared because he stopped before either of us got the feeling, and then buttoned up both of us. Of course, I went right out to the toilet and finished the job on myself, and I'm sure he did the same. There is also the recollection of the time early one morning when I was not quite awake enough to know that my father had come into the room and saw what I was doing. He didn't say anything, but came over to the bed and lifted the covers and took my hand off my cock. I was awake by that time, but pretended to be asleep. He never mentioned it. I have always thought my father enjoyed jerking himself, because I think he never got very much satisfaction from married sexual life.

He was always very careful to never let me see his prick. It became a sort of game with me to see if I could see it. He always locked the bathroom door when he went in, and I used to try to see what he was doing through the keyhole, but I never saw a thing. I think this frustration of not seeing my father or knowing how he was built has been a factor in my continued desire, even to this day, to see other cocks.

I was still experimenting. About this time a friend gave me an old bulldog. He was a gentle old thing and I used to have fun trying to put my prick up his asshole. I was never successful, so I'd turn him over on his back and play with his cock and balls till the cock came out like a red cone to a sharp point. Then I'd play with it and myself at the same time till I got mine.

I was about thirteen now and beginning to drip a little when I got the sensation. This proved to be fun. I would jerk till I came just enough to send out a little moisture, but not quite all the way. That made my prick nice and slick and heightened the sensation when I finished it off. I used to put my finger in the cum and taste it. It tasted good to me. But still the thought of ever kissing or fucking another boy never entered in. When I began to really get a load of cum with my jerking, I used to shoot it into a little tin box or small bottle so I could keep it and smell it till it dried up.

One day I was out with two other boys and we went down by the creek. The older one bet me that I couldn't shoot a load, so I took my cock out of my pants and jacked off right there to show him I did have jism. Then the other two did it and I did it again while they were jerking. While I was growing, so was my cock, and by the time I was fifteen, I was nearly six feet tall. I had measured my prick several times, having watched it grow from a little hard-on to a good six inches. It had a slight bend in it toward the left which fit my right hand perfectly. I have always thought that I jacked off so much that I produced the curve in it.

Then came the discovery that some rubber bands around it while jerking off made it feel good and gave some pressure that I thought must feel like real fucking. But I never played with girls. It was too much fun by myself and they didn't interest me that way.

Athletics were not compulsory in high school at that time. After several tries, I gave it up because I found that in the showers, seeing the other boys' cocks gave me a hard-on and it embarrassed me. I gave up athletics for sex. One day in class I saw the fellow across the aisle from me jerking off with his hand in his pocket. This was too much, so under the cover of the desk I opened my pants and jacked myself right there, letting the cum fall on the floor and wiping it around with my shoe. I'm sure that he got his in his pants about the same time. It seems to me that there was never a day that I didn't do it once or twice, and sometimes a third.

My brother and I were the only children in the family. He was five years older than me. One day I walked into his room to see him lying naked, stomach down on the floor with his ass going up and down rhythmically. He said he had found a new kind of exercise that was good for his stomach muscles, but I know he was rubbing it off on the carpet because when he stood up he had a real stiff hard-on. I did myself as he finished off his cock. This and the earlier time when he jacked me are the only two times I remember when my brother and I had sex together.

As I see it now, he had a prick much larger than mine, and what I wouldn't have given to get my hands on it. But his "exercises" gave me some ideas, and I tried rubbing it off on the carpet. Old fashioned Turkish towels made good fucking, and no doubt my mother wondered what stained all the towels. Maybe she knew, but nothing was ever said about sex at our house.

During high school I had plenty of dates and was very popular with the girls because I was a good dancer. But I never tried to fuck any of them. I just wasn't interested. After a party or a dance I'd give them a few hugs and maybe a good night kiss, then go home to jack off. One night when I was kissing a girl after a party she opened her lips and put her tongue against mine. I gave mine back to her and got a fine hard-on which went off in my pants as I rubbed against her. Even this experience wasn't any better to me than doing it myself, so I got through high school without a real fuck.

In my town, nothing was ever said or done about cock-sucking. I had never heard of it. Even in college it was not talked about in the fraternity. The nearest I ever came to it then was one weekend when there were many guests at the house and the regulars had to double up in the bunks on the sleeping porch. The proximity and the heat of the body so close to me fired me up, and I think the other fellow too, for soon I was on top of him with our arms around each other, rubbing our pricks off against the other's belly. No kissing; just hugging and rubbing. The next morning the fellow in the bunk below asked if we had fun last night, so I know he must have heard the bunk moving. I did find out a little later when one of the brothers spent the night at my house that he liked to jack off someone else as he did it himself. We managed to spend many nights together. One night he wanted me to try fucking him in the ass, but my lack of experience wasn't too helpful, and I couldn't get it in. We had no cream or Vaseline, and besides, I was afraid my parents in the next room would hear us. But several years later, after I was married, Russ and I would get together for some pleasant jerking sessions.

All this time I was very happy to use my own hands. I experimented with anything that had a hole in it about the size of my cock. Many are the milk bottles I shot into. If the bottle were warmed with hot water, the sensation was terrific. And the cardboard roller from toilet paper made a good tight fit. Then I found that bottles of certain sizes could be pushed up my asshole if I greased them a bit and put some around my hole. This felt good. I think I have run through most of the vegetable kingdom, anything shaped like a prick—carrots, bananas, Italian squash. Cucumbers make a wonderful fuck and heighten the pleasure of a good jack off. I used to try hard to reach down and take my prick in my mouth but was never able to make it, even though by this time it had grown a bit more and measured nearly seven inches.

My first cocksucking experience came on a Pullman to Chicago. There was a fellow across the aisle from me, a bit older than I, who seemed to favor my company during the day. When it came time to go to our berths, we both happened to be in the washroom when no one else was in. I've forgotten how the subject was brought up (just remember the incident), but he said if I got lonesome to come over to his birth. I got lonesome. After both of us had gone to bed, I got up and went to the washroom, and, coming back, climbed into his berth instead of mine. He was naked and on top of the covers and already had a hard-on. So I took off my pajamas and climbed on him for a good loving session. This was the first time I had had a man's tongue in my mouth, but it didn't take long to discover its delights, and very soon I was kissing him all over the head and neck as he was doing to me. He began pushing me down a bit on his body so I continued to kiss him around the shoulders and chest as he kept pushing me further down. I don't remember the size of his meat, but I do remember the exquisite thrill that went through me when I felt it against my face. I played with his balls as I kissed all around the upright prick. And, oh the deliciousness of everything when I put my lips over it. I tongued around the top of it till he gave a push and sent it further into my mouth. I was quite inexpert but he was hot as hell, and after a few pushes his load shot into my mouth. I had trouble swallowing my first load, but found that I liked it. He made no effort to go down on me so I lay beside him and jacked off into my hand and swallowed my own cum. Then I went back to my berth.

Army experience produced nothing in the way of real fucking. I didn't go out with the other fellows when they picked up girls or went to whore houses. I still got mine by myself in different ways. One I recall that seemed good was to get it almost hard, then push it down between my legs till the foreskin rubbed my asshole. By rubbing it then, I could come and feel the hot cum gush against my asshole. But the army life was so busy and I was so tired at night that my old once a day record lost out to an occasional jerk off.

After the war, marriage produced some new and pleasant thrills, but even with fucking available any night (my wife didn't like to do it in the daytime), I was still jacking off, two or three times a week between screws. During the summer my wife usually went for a visit to her home for two or three weeks. I had a fine time with Russ who lived in the same town. He spent many nights with me, but we never did more than jerk each other off. Another fellow, Jack, was a handsome guy, and I developed a terrific yen for him. We stayed together one night after being out on the town doing a little drinking. I had not thought too much about sex with Jack till this night after we were in bed, naked of course. I felt his hand come over to my meat and start a slow massage. In no time at all I was rarin' to go, but again, no sucking, just jerking each other off. Several different occasions brought the same kind of play. Another night Jack took his bath first and as he dried himself must have put some Vaseline on his asshole. When I climbed in he was curled up facing the wall. I snuggled up to him and the old meat began to swell. With almost no effort on my part, I found it well up his ass. He began to move around in evident enjoyment and I was certainly liking it. In a few strokes I was clear up to the hilt in his ass and, as I continued to fuck him, I reached around and began jerking him off. It was the first time he had ever been fucked and jerked off at the same time. We both came with a mighty heave and I went off to sleep with my cock still up his ass.

During another summer vacation I enjoyed my first rimming. A friend was spending the night and we began with a good loving. Soon both of us were hot. He went down on me and gave me a good tonguing around my balls and crotch. He worked down to the hole and when his lips touched it, I almost blew from the exhilaration. He pushed back my legs till they were against my stomach and the hole was exposed. He seemed to bore right in and his tongue went in further than I have ever been able to make mine go in an ass. I have tried, but was never able to make my tongue as stiff as his, but it was thrilling. Being thoroughly lubricated, he had no trouble entering my now quivering asshole with his meat for a wonderful fuck, so good that I came at the same time he did just by body rubbing.

Some time or other I found that a good heavy rubber band twisted around the base of a hard cock would hold the hard-on indefinitely and I have kept it that way an hour or more. With a good tight rubber band, a stiff well-oiled piece of meat, a warmed bottle just a little tight in size to make me increase the effort to get it in, and a cock-shaped something up my asshole, I can transport myself into delirium of ecstasy well beyond any experience I have had in normal fucking.

Long live a stiff prick and a good right hand!

MORE

The following experiences may not be in chronological order like the first set, but there are still many interesting and exciting episodes that were not included in the first paper.

One time, before the cocksucking period, I was indulging with a friend in a hot and passionate, naked loving session. Eventually my stiff prick found its way between his tightly clenched legs and I was on the way to a good dry fuck. He had more experience than I and suggested that I finish by putting some mentholated shaving cream on my meat. I thoroughly covered my hard-on with the cream and went back to work. It was a delicious sensation. Just enough menthol to add additional prickles to what I was already feeling. He too enjoyed it as the menthol rubbed into the sensitive skin of his crotch and on his balls. So we both came in a flurry of excitement. Later on I tried the same idea in jerking off and found it good. I have since tried many other creams and lotions and find the most exquisite orgasm comes from a lathering of Gleem toothpaste. It is stronger than shaving cream and a good lathering till the whole stiff cock is covered with sudsy slickness, coupled with the movement of the warm hand to bring out the menthol tingles, is something not to be missed.

One time when we had both worked ourselves just about to come, another friend suggested that I sit on his prick. So after greasing his meat and my asshole, I sat down on top of him, facing his face and shoulders. He had rather a long one but not as thick and it went in with ease and gusto. I was enjoying the fuck while he jacked me off. He was limber enough to reach down with his head and take my cock in his mouth while he continued to fuck my ass. Boy! That was a sensation! To be fucked and sucked at the same time. Wow! One that was even better than that was a three way. The loving got pretty wild till you didn't know whose cock you had in your mouth or hand or who was ass-fucking who. But we ended up with me on my side in the middle being fucked by a beautiful piece of meat from behind and doing a 69 with the one in front of me. The one behind can push his cock in to the hilt while those in front can take advantage of uninhibited hard-ons and take them clear down to the balls. Even choking a bit on the size and depth of the cock you have in your mouth adds to the pleasure of the loads of cum that are being swallowed.

I used to have a seventy mile drive on weekends in the summer, going up late Saturday in the dark and coming back very early Monday morning. There was never too much of a hurry either way, so I didn't drive too fast. As soon as I was on the open road I undid my pants and took out my cock and started playing with myself. It didn't take long to get a good hard-on—the regular vibration of the motor and the road helped, and I would jack myself till I almost came, then give it a cooling off time and start again. With no hurry to shoot, jacking off can be a great pleasure. Tensions build up and the final blow is a burst of delirium. When I jerk off now, I still try to make it last a long time.

On one of these trips while I still had my pants unzipped, I picked up a sailor. It didn't take long for me, already hot from jerking, to bring the talk around to fucking. He had been on the base for some time and was also hot. We each took out our pricks and played with the others for miles. Several times one or the other would almost shoot, but we held off. He had a nice piece of meat, not unusual in size, but very virile-looking. Somehow or other I haven't met with any of the story book size or the prize exhibits. I drove him to my house before I went to work. He wanted to fuck up the ass so we both stripped and I greased my hole and his cock. We both had a good fuck with my legs wrapped around his back so we could kiss and love at the same time. I remember his southern accent, when he was about ready to shoot.

He gasped, "Oh, it's fixin' to come. It's fixin' to come!"

That added to my fun, so we both shot at the same time. Of course, I covered his belly with my cum, but the slipperiness between us made it even better. And when it was over, I had more pleasure licking at my own cum from his stomach. We showered together and had more loving during the process, but no more comes. So I took him where he could get the bus he wanted and then went to work myself.

I have found that I can enjoy myself in the shower bath too. The shower stall is large enough for us to move around freely and the shower head can be adjusted to a fine brisk spray. Standing up I can hold my cock under one of the sprays and the tingle on the foreskin soon has me getting a hard-on. Then I hold my upright prick against my belly and let the spray hit the underside of the sensitive foreskin. I very gradually draw the skin down over the head in the spray. The sensation of the slowly moving skin and the tingle of the spray gives a wonderful feeling. I can only do this a very few times before I shoot. Sometimes I sit down on the floor facing the shower with my limp prick against my belly and let the spray do all the work. That sensitive spot soon gives me a throbbing prick, and before long I am shooting without having touched my cock. In that somewhat crouched position and with the warm water falling on me, I seem to have a heightened come.

I have heard of but never seen mental masturbation. A friend knows a young guy who in a very few minutes can produce a good come just by thinking about it. There is probably the stimulation of another naked body and no doubt jacking off to watch, but in a short time a completely limp prick becomes hard and throbbing and soon shoots a load of cum without having been touched. I have tried to do this, as I have tried most everything I have heard about, but I need some manipulation or touching to produce the goods.

While I am writing this I am drooling like mad into my shorts and know that if I were in a place where I could do it, the lubrication and about three strokes would shoot me off.

I will never forget my first night in Chicago, where I had gone on a scholarship to a private teacher. It was on the way there in the Pullman that I enjoyed my first cocksucking, and I arrived all fired up to try anything. The teacher met me at the train and said we were to meet some of his friends. Coming from a small town where there were no saloons, I was surprised to be taken in the "family" entrance of one where we found several women and men sitting around a table waiting for us. There were drinks and dinner and then we, the two of us, went to my teacher's home where I was to stay till I found a place of my own. I was tired and ready to go to bed but while I was in the tub, Arthur, the teacher, came in and casually looked me over to the extent that my prick began to swell. Again the "lonesome" routine.

If I was lonely, come into his room. Naturally, I did, and the loving began. He kissed me all over from the top of my head to my toes, but not touching my prick with his mouth. The poor thing was standing as straight as it could, considering the curve in it, and was being brushed by his body and arms as he moved around. He finally came up the inside of my legs and worked his mouth into my crotch. By this time I was giving him all the help I could and spread my legs to enjoy every bit of it. He came up and pulled the foreskin up over the head and very gently took it in his mouth and just held it that way for a while. Then, very slowly he forced the skin down and as slowly, bit by bit, went down on the whole cock. By the time he hit the bottom I was wild and shot a load that I hope gave him all he wanted. After I had rested a while he began again and the same process was repeated with the same results. Then I rolled him on his back and tried, in my inexperience, to do for him what he had done for me. It must have been good because he had a big come. Three more times that night he sucked me off. I think that is my record, five in one night. But don't forget, I was only twenty at the time. He taught me many things besides the instruction I had gone to Chicago to get.

My experience and technique in cocksucking developed very rapidly there, and I was soon able to give as good a blow job as the next one.

I realized later, when I knew more about such things, that the men and women I met on my first night in Chicago were homos: both Lesbian and male. Probably they all looked me over; this tall, quite good-looking young fellow from the West, with lustful ideas. If they ever got together for orgies, I was never invited to join them, but it would have been a good way to add to my education. I guess they thought I was Arthur's personal property.

An interesting sidelight to all this is that I left Chicago, returning to the West Coast where I have been ever since. I did not see Arthur for nearly twenty years, then when he was here on a visit we got together. He was occupying the apartment of a friend, and I went to see him. After one bourbon our clothes were off and we were locked in a wonderful embrace. He had never rimmed me before, nor I him. After he had kissed and sucked my ass with great pleasure to me, he took over on my hard-on with the old slow technique, and once more, by the time he got to the bottom of my prick, I shot the wad. Gosh! What a feeling! Just once down the length of it, very slowly, building up an agony of pleasure, till the cock is completely inside his mouth, and can't hold the orgasm any longer; then the release makes shooting stars and crashing cymbals all over the place. As experienced as I have become, I have never been able to give anyone else this particular exquisite way of coming. So I did my best for him, finger fucking his ass while I sucked his prick. After this we rested in each other's arms for a while till we were hot again. This time we did a regular 69, which was also fun. His cock was short but quite thick, and just a wonderful mouthful. With our pricks in each other's mouths we rolled around, first one on top, then the other. With pauses to take in a mouthful of balls and then go on down to the asshole for kissing, we kept this up for some time and both got back to the 69 position in time to come together. Whew! But two of those comes was enough for me, such a long time after the first record of five in one night.

These are a few of the highlights of a long and pleasurable sex life. I will continue to jack off with my rubber bands and other helps, finger fuck myself or use a bottle or some other imaginary prick, suck a cock or fuck an ass, or be sucked or fucked when the occasion arises. Right now I am so worked up that I am going to the bathroom and give myself a few good jerks, take the cum in my hand and swallow it so I can taste my own fun.

CHAPTER ELEVEN
HOT ROD

Again youth and innocence is the basis for this short erotic piece. The author has included another favorite tidbit of perverseness...urophilia (the fascination with urine). This is not actually as uncommon as some may think. In the world of homosexuality, the "golden shower queen" is far from a rarity. Although it is considered a masochistic trait, it is a practice employed by many individuals.

The following piece concerns a sadistic ex-serviceman who deflowers a young boy of seventeen. The ending of the story hints on there being a sequel to it, although no evidence thereof has been discovered to date. Again a very vague reference to heterosexuality is introduced as a lead-in to the sexual depravities participated in by the two boys. The story holds true to the usual structure necessary to the erotic short story...its pacing is fast and obscene. No attention is given to unnecessary detail and no mention is made of anything that does not possess erotic or sexual content. It is told to excite the reader and the author is successful in his purpose.

* * * * * *

Tom was lying on his back under his hot rod when he heard the roar of a motorcycle coming up the driveway. Just the delivery boy, he thought, as his greasy hands reached up into the dark undersides of the car. He heard the cleats on the cement drive and a voice say, "Where in hell do you want this stuff left?" Tom slid out from under the car, raised himself on one knee and looked at the stranger.

The boy standing in the garage was tall, blond, and broad of shoulder. His tight T-shirt disappeared into an equally tight pair of faded Levi's that hung carelessly over worn motorcycle boots. The boys looked at each other for a moment; the delivery boy held a large box of groceries.

"Mom's out, just put them up on the service porch and I'll put the things away later."

The boy turned and disappeared.

Tom pulled himself up, reached for a soiled rag and stood wiping his greasy hands as the boy returned in the doorway.

"I dumped the things on the porch like you said. Christ, it's hot today! Say, that's quite a jalopy you've got. You really fixed it up great." He examined the car and turned to gaze at Tom. Tom was seventeen years old and had black curly hair, and an infectious smile. The delivery boy remarked, "Christ, you're just a kid. I thought you were an older guy."

Tom stood up, barefooted and bare to the waist. His Levi's hung so low on his narrow hips that it seemed as if any small movement would drop them to his ankles. He only laughed at the remark and said, "I guess you're a grandfather!"

The other boy smiled and said, "My name is Jim. I'm all of twenty-five and just finished a stretch in the Navy. I'm delivering for old man Smith this summer and right now I've got to take a piss like crazy. Got a head anywhere around?"

Tom jerked his thumb in the direction of the corner of the garage and said, "You can use that old sink over there, I always take a leak in it when I don't want to go into the house."

The other boy dragged his boots across the cement in the designated direction. Tom heard the exclamations as the boy said, "Man, where did you get these pictures?"

Tom laughed and said, "Pretty jazzy, aren't they? They were here when we moved in and Mom keeps telling me to rip them off the wall, but I keep putting it off as I like to look at them."

"Christ, I don't blame you; they're pretty damned hot! Boy, this one of Marilyn Monroe...what a body!" Tom heard the thick stream of piss hit the porcelain bowl and unconsciously walked over to the emergency head. He leaned against the wall and observed the older boy who stood with his legs spread apart. His jeans seemed to be painted a faded blue over the curve of his tight ass. His left hand was on his hip and his right was holding his cock. The amber liquid continued to splatter in the basin and the boy went on making remarks about the semi-nude pin-up pictures. Tom became aware that the evacuation sounds had stopped, yet the boy's right hand moved back and forth as he shook his cock.

"Christ, I could use a piece of tail right now." Tom's mouth felt dry and his face felt hot and flushed. He leaned against the wall and watched the muscles of the boy's rear end flex as the right arm kept up a slow steady motion. Tom ran his own hand up between his firm legs and felt the large erection that had been throbbing there for some time. The boy looked over his shoulder and saw Tom's face flushed in embarrassment with his hand outstretched over the large swelling in his pants.

"Christ, not you too? You ought to be used to these pictures." The boy turned his body so he was in profile. His left hand still remained on his hip and Tom finally saw the huge erection as his right hand slid up and down the large shaft. The boy stood with his legs spread apart and his body arched forward with the big head of his cock sliding in and out of his large fist.

"Boy, how I'd love to shove my joint in the mouth of that babe's cunt." Tom's legs felt weak as hot fluid dripped down his left leg. He watched the dark stain grow larger on his Levi's. He licked his dry lips and took a deep breath to steady himself.

The boy stood sizing him up and through half-closed eyes said, "Christ, looks like you got a man-sized weapon on you, boy." Tom was speechless with embarrassment and emotion. The boy answered, "Close that goddamn garage door...it's too bright in here."

Tom, as if in a trance, walked to the door and closed it. He then turned around and saw the boy standing there...He dropped his Levi's and they hung over his boots; one hand was fondling the huge pair of balls as the other hand was now rubbing a shiny fluid over the dilated rim of the big cock.

"Come here a minute and feel how hard this is."

As Tom approached, the boy took Tom's hand and put it on his cock. The boy's hand was slowly unbuttoning Tom's fly. Tom felt his Levi's drop to the floor and the other guy said, "Kick 'em off," as he pulled Tom close to him. They stood there rubbing bodies together and the older boy was feeling Tom's body all over. Tom's hand was fondling the older boy's large balls and stroking his big tool. Tom heard him say, "Better go easy on that monster, it's loaded and hot as a pistol. How do you like it? Can you take it all the way down?"

Tom stood shaking from excitement and was too worked up to answer as the older boy stood massaging the swollen head of his large tool. The boy milked it forward and large wads of cum oozed out. The boy said, "You'd knock a babe up before you ever got your gun. I never saw a guy with such a load." Then Tom heard the boy say, "Go ahead and take it," and he felt himself pulled forward and down.

Tom sank to his knees. He looked at the boy's scuffed motor-cycle boots and saw the short blond hair on his muscular legs and thick thighs. He smelled a heavy masculine odor emitting from the boy's body as his eyes rested on the huge erection just before his face. The big boy cupped Tom's head in his hands and pushed his torso forward. He forced the large head between Tom's half-parted lips. "Oh! Christ man, tongue me, lick my balls, get between my legs, give me a bath."

Tom was now in a feverish emotion. Slowly, in and out of Tom's eager mouth, the boy worked his big shaft. Tom began to play with his own cock and balls. The boy growled, "Go ahead, beat hell out of that big piece of meat. I want to watch you shoot your wad! Shoot it on my boots. That ought to shine 'em up!" Tom was so hot that he allowed the boy to screw him in the mouth as he swallowed the large cock down his throat.

He felt the swelling grow when the boy groaned as Tom applied suction over the swollen head of the big tool. Tom's own rod shot forth load after load up the boy's legs, covering the boots. The boy looked down and moaned, "Man look at that load!", as he released his own large discharge down Tom's throat. Tom gulped and swallowed fast. As the shots ran down his throat and out of the corners of his mouth and down his chin, he sank back on his haunches, breathing rapidly and wiped his mouth on the back of his hand.

The older boy stood with his legs still spread apart and said, "You really liked it, didn't you?" Tom didn't answer, but looked down at his cupped right hand that contained a full ounce of thick liquid. "Well, hell, answer me," snarled the older boy as he dug a heavy boot into Tom's rib. "You heard me tell you to shoot your load all over my boots, didn't you?"

"Yeah," he replied huskily, "I guess so."

"Well, I mean it! Rub that jism into the leather with your hands!" Tom held the boot with one hand and smeared the sticky juice with his other hand over the boot. "Now use the rag and polish hell out of 'em." Tom felt a mixed emotion of fright and repulsion, yet he was strongly attracted to the masculine dominance of the older boy. He stepped over to pick up a cloth as the boy leaned back on the fender of the car. He just stood with his legs spread apart and looked down at the still semi-erection of his own big tool. Tom saw how it looked, even bigger glistening with the saliva and cum that covered the large tool and ran down into the tight blond crotch hairs. Tom held the rag and, on his knees, began to polish the boot. The boy moved his other leg so that his boot rested between Tom's legs with the sole of it pressing down on Tom's cock and balls.

As he polished away, the motion of his own body coupled with the movements of the boot in his crotch caused his cock to swell. He looked up and saw that the boy had another full erection and was now massaging the head of his cock. "Looks like it isn't dead yet; why not wet it for me? Go ahead and spit on the head of it."

Tom cleared his throat and moistened up a mouth full of spit and let it drip over the head of the big tool. The older boy began to work the spit up and down the shaft and around the big head. "Well, hell, go ahead on the other boot." As Tom now began on the second boot, he looked down and saw his own tool at a full erection and standing straight up between his squatting legs. He polished away vigorously as the heavy boot began to fascinate him. The older boy began to relate a tale that happened on shipboard late at night between two sailors and himself. He elaborated on the happenings, describing incidents to the most intimate details. Tom worked faster on the boot and said, "Go on, tell me more," as he ran his hands up the boy's legs and played with his huge, swollen balls.

The older boy now had his legs wrapped around the kneeling boy and was treading the boots up and down over the young body. The air was heavy with the smell of polished leather and of the odor of the two bodies emitting sweat, and sex. Tom was now on his hands and knees, licking the legs and balls as he heard the boy say, "Do you like this kind of sex?"

"Gosh yes, I've never been so hot in all my life."

The boy sat back and put his boot on Tom's shoulder and rubbed it against the cheek of his face. Tom was beside himself. As he smelled the thick leather of the masculine boy's odor, he began to play with himself again. The older boy sat on the running board of the hot rod with his balls hanging down between his thick thighs. "If you do as I say, we can have lots of fun. How about it?"

"I'll do anything you want me to, if we can do this again."

"Can you take it, and not tell anybody?"

"Yes, I'll try to do what you want me to do."

"Well, lie down on your back." Tom lay down on the floor with his hands behind his head and his big erection standing like a flagpole, and the older boy stepped across him with his legs spread and stood over him. "Okay, go ahead and let me watch you play with that big cock. See how high you can shoot your gun in the air, but don't come until I say to. Okay?"

Tom watched as the muscular boy stood over his outstretched body. He played with his own erection and teased his big piece of meat until he was in a frenzy. The cement floor felt cool on his burning body as he writhed and rubbed his back and small ass against the cold cement. He watched the older boy slide the wide belt out of his Levi's. The belt curved through the air and cut against Tom's body with a cracking sound. Tom winced and groaned. The belt cut through the air again and again, leaving red whip marks across Tom's chest and legs.

Tom twisted and turned over, leaving his back and small ass exposed to the steady blows. As the black snake cut across his ass, he was more and more sexually stimulated. The heavy belt cut through the skin in places leaving long, red marks, the older boy dropped his arms to his side and stood panting, the sweat streaming down his face and said, "Okay, roll over on your back." Tom complied to this wish and saw the lustful look on the handsome face. The boy said, "How about a shower?" His cock stood out as a swollen erection and Tom saw a yellow arc of fluid as it shot into the air and splattered over his body.

Tom was covered with the warm piss. The boy squatted low over Tom's face as the fluid bathed his body and face. The older boy moved forward so that his large tool was even with Tom's face and bathed it with amber fluid. "Go ahead and drink it!" Tom opened his mouth and the boy filled it for him with his warm piss. The liquid stopped as the guy wildly began to work his big tool back and forth. Tom just watched in a hypnotic state as the load struck him full in the face and ran down into his open mouth. The boy stood up and put his hand on Tom's chest as Tom got his load off, again and again.

The boy wiped his hands and dangling cock on the car rag, pulled on the skin-tight Levi's, and buckled the wide black torture belt back into place. "Christ, I'm late as hell for work...I'll get canned! Listen, I'll be back next Tuesday, and from here on in, you'd better be around. We'll pick up here where we left off. I want to fuck the hell out of that little ass till it bleeds."

As he strolled out of the garage, Tom rolled over on his side and began to sob as he realized that he was lost forever, but he was already beginning to look forward to the following Tuesday and to the feel of that hand, masculine body.

CHAPTER TWELVE
INVITATION TO THE RANCH

This story takes us "out West," to a ranch that provides the setting for all sorts of sexuality, mostly in the form of orgies. But despite the difference in setting, it combines all the standard elements of the *Tijuana Bible Story*. We have incestuous hanky-panky; an inexperienced young hero with the predictably large endowments; an entire bunkhouse full of rugged, ultra-masculine men, all of whom are presumably bisexual; an abundance of super-large and ultra-potent male organs; an absolute lack of scruples, morals, conscience, guilt, or anything else that might impair our young heathens from indulging themselves freely; only token resistance to various seductions, followed by warmhearted acceptance.

Like the uniformed males described in previous adventures, the cowboy enjoys a certain appeal in this material. Indeed, he has recently become especially popular. The so-called Loon Trilogy *(Song of the Loon, Song of Aaron,* and *Listen, the Loon Sings)* made the cowboy and the Western setting highly popular in gay fiction. The result—cowboy erotica—was surely inevitable. But the truth is, the cowboy has always enjoyed his place in these stories. With bowed legs, leathery skin, rugged odor, he has appeared time and time again as a sex symbol—sometimes without his knowledge.

* * * * * *

One Saturday afternoon my brother Art called me upstairs to his room. Our folks had gone to town shopping and we were to meet them at our grandparents later for dinner. As I entered his room, I thought it strange the way he had asked me to his room. He was stripping his clothes off and I thought he was going to shower, but he just plopped across his bed on his back, kicking his heels into the air. He had been working out and this was the first time I had noticed his strong back muscles. His butt was firm and a line was started where his swimming suit left off.

"Sit down, I want to talk to you," he said, as he petted the bed beside him. "How are you making out with Annie next door; are you getting into her?"

I was seventeen and my brother would soon be twenty, but he had never discussed his sex life with me. Maybe he was hot for Annie himself, so maybe I had better be careful.

"What makes you think it's possible?" I asked. "She looks like she really has hot pants for you." He turned over on his back and I saw he had been holding down his hard cock. This was the first time I had seen his tool excited, and even though it didn't seem quite as long as mine, it was plenty of cock. He had been doing a lot of growing up since going away to college.

"I don't think Ann would like my discussing her with you. Maybe you should do your own investigating," I answered. I had had some rather hot nights with her on the back seat of her father's car the past winter, and it seemed as if she was always the first one to suggest sex.

"Her whole family looks sexy to me—especially her brother," Art replied. "He looks like the most fun in bed."

This was a strange remark, I thought, but I just shelved it for the time being. Art was stroking his cock and playing around with his balls by now, and this made me kind of hot, just watching someone else beating his meat. My jockey shorts began to fill up with my stiff prick. I knew I did not have the build he had, but I knew I could better the build he had in the cock department by at least an inch in each direction. Besides, I knew I could go off five times in a twenty-four hour period.

"This fucker sure needs a beating," Art said, giving his prick some real fast strokes. "You don't know where I could get a good blow job now do you?"

I watched him slowly and shook my head no. "I thought I would go and see Annie, and maybe she could find a quiet spot for a good screw before meeting the folks." As I stood up to leave, Art grabbed my meat.

"Stick around, I want to talk to you some more," he said. By now he was giving that hot rod of his some might fancy strokes and his balls seemed to be tightening up around his belly.

"I have a chance to go up to a ranch for a while this summer, and thought you might like to go along. That is if you think you would have a good time," Art said. "There'll be no women around, so you'll really miss your Annie, but I think you'll really have some fun."

"Sure, it sounds good to me, I can always find something to do with a stiff prick," I said.

He then jumped up from the bed and ran for the bathroom, swinging his cock from side to side. He probably was heading to the bathroom to unload his cum there. I stood up, pulled my stiff rod up against my belly as best I could, and left him to his own desires.

We took the invitation offered to us to go to the ranch for a couple of months during summer vacation. I could use some fresh air and exercise before starting to college in the fall, and Art needed to build up his energy for his senior year's activities.

The ranch was for cattle herding and was a big operation. There were twelve hired hands plus the owner and his two sons handling the work. We were met at the bus station by the two boys, ages fourteen and sixteen, in a big station wagon that smelled like the last load was overripe bullshit. At first glance they looked like two men. Their faces were so tan from being out of doors year round and their hair was sun-bleached like ripened wheat. Since it was a very hot day, they were sweating freely, and as soon as we left town, they both stripped off their shirts. They must have been wrestling, from the looks of those rippling muscles across their backs and arms. Their Levi's looked painted on their thick hard legs. Both of them had a habit of grabbing their crotch as if they had hot pants all the time.

"Think we will get along for the summer with you two city guys?" asked Hugo, the younger.

"Shut up, Hugo," said Lem, the other hand. "You know what Dad warned you about trying to pick a fuss."

This didn't sound like a very friendly beginning, but I thought both kids might prove to be a pair of pretty nice guys after we got to know them. I was hot and dusty and soon my shirt was soaked and so was Art's. Our new Levi's scratched our legs and as we didn't have our cowpoke hats, our heads were hot too. It was a long ride back to the ranch, and the road was plenty rough too.

"We can jump into the horse trough," Hugo said, "that'll cool you down right quick. My cock and balls are as wet now as when the calf gets through sucking them."

"Don't be giving away our secrets too soon, Hugo," laughed Lem. "You'll get them horny and they'll spend all their time with the calf." Hugo got a kick out of this little joke and grabbed Lem by the balls. Lem was driving and swerved off the road a second.

"You're not so cool yourself; that damn old cock is so hard just thinking about it. Look at it." And with that he jerked Lem's meat out of his pants. It was about twice as thick as mine and more lengthy than Art's. Farming sure developed cocks on husky kids of sixteen. Hugo was called "Huge," and we soon found out why. He knelt on the seat facing Lem and ripped his pants down, to let his thick long rod flip straight out.

"Let the calf suck this," he yelled, "and he'll never go back to that stunted prick of yours." This equipment sticking out in front of this fourteen-year-old would do credit to any full-grown man. Art was quietly taking in the whole show and I noticed his pants were bulging in the crotch. I knew that my dick was hard too.

Finally we pulled into a white-gated drive and up to a yard

filled with cars. Behind a large clump of trees was the adobe house, white and cool-looking with dark green shutters. "Leave your bags there and I'll show you the water trough," Hugo said; he had already unfastened his pants, and now he took off toward the barn. Behind it was a long concrete trough, about six feet wide, next to a windmill. Lem had stripped and jumped in bare-ass. He splashed around with lots of noise. Hugo just took off his boots and jumped in with his pants on.

"It shrinks them up and they keep you cool while drying off," Hugo stated. So we followed suit and jumped in with our new Levi's on. Art was very active now and dove under Lem several times. He finally took off his pants and threw them over the side; evidently they were rubbing his stiff prick. We all played grab-ass, but I noticed Art could hardly keep his hands off Hugo's big cock.

A ringing bell at the house called us in and we found that by the time we reached the back door, we were dry enough to be presented to the boy's parents. After lunch, we laid around and napped on the porch while the boys did their regular chores. Our bags had been put in the bunkhouse where we were to sleep. This was a long, low dormitory where the hired hands slept.

After dinner and a couple of television shows, bedtime was announced. It seemed early to us—but then life starts early on a ranch. Lem and Hugo led us by flashlight to the bunkhouse and after we were settled in our bunks, they took off for the house. Art seemed disappointed that they didn't stay and sleep with the hired help. We had met several of the men, some in bed, some showering, and some just lying around reading or talking. They all seemed rather young, like pretty good Joes—rough, but not unpleasant. Art and I had an upper and lower near the door. We shed our strange new clothing and slipped between the sheets. Not much more than ten minutes passed when the lights went out. Then everyone went to bed and the room became quiet.

Later I was awakened by a clatter of boots and muffled voices, lots of giggling and shushing. I finally was able to make out a group of five men right opposite my bunk bed, and when I heard a girl cry out, I raised up on one elbow. Art reached down to wake me, but I told him I was awake by pushing up on the bottom of his mattress. By now I could see better in the dark and could see the girl had been stripped and her bare tits were sticking straight out; her hair fell over her shoulder as someone was pulling her shoes back on and someone else was tying her arms over her head to the top bunk just across the aisle from our bunk. She spread her legs a little and moaned very softly. Then he put his hands on her ass and started pumping it to her. He fell onto her, shoving his cock into her, with all his clothes on, including his hat. About two minutes of that movement and he groaned and stopped, as he had evidently shot his load. When he backed away, I could see his still hard, wet prick hanging out of his pants. He was pushed to one side and someone took his place immediately, only this one had taken off his shirt at least. Before he could finish, he was interrupted by a short fellow, dressed only in his boots and a stiff prick. It was amazing how well I could see in the dark after my eyes had become adjusted to it. This guy tried to shove his rod right up between the other's fellow's legs. Well he got shoved back on his ass for that attempt, but pulled himself up near our bunk. Art must have been beating his meat like mad for the bunk was shaking, but I didn't blame him as I had thrown the sheet back off my flaming cock too.

The short cowboy sure had a man-sized cock and held it as if he were afraid it was going to pop off before he could get to the girl. He sat down on the bed and evidently wasn't able to see as well as I, for he felt around to see if there was anyone in the bed and his hand brushed my stiff prick. His hand stopped and he felt the full length of it, running his hand up and down a couple of times. Over my shoulder, I could see someone else was now knocking a hard cock into that poor cunt, but this time her lover had dropped his pants down over his knees.

Art jumped down and stood in the aisle between the bunks near the fellow beating my meat; he stopped to see who was there, and when he saw Art's hard cock, sticking straight out in front of him, he took it in one hand and held mine in the other, giving them a fine pumping. Art stepped closer and the guy took Art's cock in his mouth, in order that he could beat his own meat awhile. No one was paying any attention to us as they seemed too interested in their turn at the girl tied to the bunk. Watching the guy blowing Art got me so hot that I thought my balls were going to burst and as if he knew what my trouble was, the cowboy stopped sucking on Art long enough to plunge down on my throbbing shaft. Pow...that was it, and come I did. I was sure my backbone had dissolved and ran out through my cock. I was so pooped I just flopped back on the bed and drifted off to sleep. I didn't wake until early in the morning and it seemed like hundreds of boots were stomping around in the faint dawn. The cowpokes were going to work and I had dozed off during the height of their sexy fiasco. DAMN.

When we saw the two boys at noon, they offered us a ride back to the place where they had been repairing fences, if we wanted to help. Art and I jumped on the backs of the horses that Lem and Hugo rode bareback. I rode with Hugo, and Art with Lem. I found out that swimming in my Levi's had made them fit tight and my cock sure got polished with that tight material, rubbing it every bounce the horse made. It was quite a distance to the section and I found myself ramming those firm buttocks of Hugo's with a stiff prick. I had one arm around him to keep from slipping off the horse and his heart was beating very fast. We raced with Lem and Art for a way and soon were dripping with sweat. Slowing down, Hugo reached around and grabbed my hard cock.

"That's a mighty long prick to try to shove in my ass," Hugo said. "You'd better aim it in some other direction if we are to get to the fence this afternoon." With that he twisted my cock back against my belly, none too gently. Then he took his hand, grabbed mine that was holding onto him, and shoved it down over his bulging damp crotch.

"Hang onto this for a while, my tits are getting tender." His overgrown rod was sticking straight up out of his pants. It was about the size of the pommel on the saddle, but longer. "This is the way Lem and I ride for hours. Now take your cock out and lay it straight up between us. You'll ride easier."

This was the situation when Lem and Art rode up beside us. I noticed Art had both hands on Lem's bare hot prick. Lem smiled and seemed to be enjoying himself greatly. "I've already shot a load with those soft hands of your brother's wrapped around my dong. Looks like you two were having some fun too."

We had come to the spot where the boys had been working. We had ridden into sort of a shallow canyon with small caves up under the gentle sloping hills beyond the sage. After an hour of repairing the broken spots and digging new holes for fence posts, Hugo suggested we knock off and go up into the caves and relax. He stripped off his clothes, leaving his boots on, and hung the sweat-soaked clothes on the fence to dry. He must have done this before as he was tanned all over and had no swimming suit line like Art and me.

His equipment looked strange slapping against his legs, completely out of place when you saw it attached to a hairless youth. It must have been difficult for his mother to change his diapers when he was little.

The others just took off their shirts, but I found my Levi's tight so I stripped down too. I hung them alongside Hugo's to dry and pulled my shoes back on to navigate over the brush. The cool sand in the cave felt good on my bare sweaty ass as I sat down. Soon we were spread out in all positions, sound asleep.

Before long I was awakened by a snapping twig and got up. Lem and Art were lying about ten feet from me and Art was going down on Lem's stiff cock. This was the first time I had seen Art do this, but I'm sure from the way he was going at it, it wasn't the first time for him. Lem was raised up on his elbows watching the performance, and I rather thought it was his first blow job experience. He had been off once not too long before, so Art was having to work a little to get another load so soon. I saw that Hugo had wakened and was beating his big thick meat, just watching.

Suddenly he blew his load all over his belly, and I think this was the first time I had ever seen another guy come. It was really a lot of thick cream that spurted up out of the huge head and ran back down over his balls. I was watching him from below a bit, and it made the head of his cock look bigger than the head of his body. Lem noticed Hugo was shooting his load on his belly, reached down and took his cock from Art's mouth, jumped up, ripped his pants off and flopped down on Hugo's wet creamy belly. Art followed him over and with some protesting and a difficulty, he finally got his prick into Lem's ass. Hugo was getting the weight of both of them on his well-spent prick and balls, so he started wiggling his ass as if he were getting his kicks all over again.

I grabbed my meat, stood up over them and began beating it, and I was too hot to shoot it off now. Hugo motioned me closer to him and pulled me down to my knees and began to jack it off for me. When Art saw this he pounded Lem's ass harder and with his eyes glued on my enlarged cock getting a real hand job he gave one final plunge and filled Lem with a load of hot cum. I started shooting all over Lem's back and Hugo's side, which excited them all so much more that Lem's squirming around so much knocked Art off and he fell limp into the sand. From the looks of his soft cock he had surely given Lem a fucking.

We hadn't had time to tell Lem and Hugo about what we had been doing in the bunkhouse, but after all, we were going to be around for a while, and we were in hopes we would have lots more to tell them later.

One night we did have another experience to add to our list. After TV we all went to bed in a very quiet bunkhouse. It was after the lights were out, so we stumbled around a little but didn't realize that there were many sleeping in that night. We heard no voices and didn't see any flashlights, so we were soon asleep. I hadn't any more than settled down when I heard someone say, "Shove over Mac, I'm getting in." It was a very rough voice and so was the guy speaking. He just gathered me into his arms, filling up most of the bed and held me against his horsy-smelling body. Soon I felt his prick climb up between us and he started biting my ears. Then he nuzzled down into my neck and then was on my tits. His hands were stroking my back and buttocks. Then he reached down between us and put his hot rod up tight between my legs. He then pulled my stiffened cock up against my belly and massaged the swelling head. I was being raped. I found I liked this very masculine approach. He kept moving around and I found myself down under him stretched out on my belly. "It's time I put this prick of mine where you want it most," he said.

"Not there, big boy, that's virgin territory," I protested. But he continued rubbing the head of it up between the squirming cheeks of my ass, with his other hand stroking my ramming rod and firm balls. He spit on his fingers and gently pressed one thick calloused finger into the entrance above my tender sphincter, slowly massaging the tight muscles. Finally, by using lots more spit on the head of his cock, he was able to get just that much more into that little hole.

"Just relax a little, and I'll not hurt you," he whispered in my ear. He ran his tongue around and into my ears, still pushing his weighty stiff rod that he was trying to pierce me with. This was too much for his passions all at once, and I felt a hot rush of cum shoot into me and his big hand closed down over my prick and balls. I let fly a load that landed up by my pillow. "Thanks, kid, I'll be back for lots more of that," he muttered, as he quietly slipped out of the bed.

A rhythm soon started and he got the point of rolling and plunging, like he loved every minute of it. I hoped he would blow his wad soon as I felt the grease wearing thin. He finally grabbed my cock and balls, hooked his chin over my shoulder, and let his load charge into me. His cock was swimming in cum and by now he had filled my guts with at least a couple of quarts. Until now I hadn't noticed that we had an audience and one of the spectators was the little cowboy that had given me my first blow job. When he saw that my partner had gotten his off, he pushed us both over on our sides and went down on my cock, while the other rod was still in my ass. The little cowboy went to work sliding up and down my prick and playing with my balls at the same time. Another spectator was Art. He walked up close to the little cowboy, spit on his cock and started it home. His hot cock was soon up the ass of the guy working on me and when he touched bottom, the little cowboy nearly bit off my cock with excitement, but soon was most enthusiastically sucking better than ever. The rough one that had just fucked me was asleep by now, with his cock still lying in its own cum. It was soft enough by now that it felt good in there and with this wonderful treatment of my own rod, I unleashed a torrent of hot lava down the little one's throat. He straightened up after that and took Art's cock in deeper. His own cock was throbbing and I reached out to give him a hand job while Art bent over and screwed him in the ass. When Art came, the little one got so excited that he shot out all over my chest and arms. The little party had ended and everyone crept back to his own bunk....

CHAPTER THIRTEEN
FAREWELL PARTY

The following account of a young handsome prisoner's farewell party is written solely for the satisfaction of a sadistic mind. The sex is not as detailed as the brutality connected with it. Pain and suffering seem to occupy the major niche of the writer's structure. It makes little sense and has no other purpose but to sate the sadistic reader's appetite for brutality. Although it is obviously pure fantasy, it does give insight to the character of its creator.

* * * * * * *

The husky teen-ager stood in the center of the windowless basement room facing three uniformed men. Like all the prisoners, he was barefoot and wore a blue denim workshirt and trousers. He was ruggedly good-looking with black, curly hair and clear, dark eyes, and his face was well-tanned.

"Well, Rocky, this is the day we let you out."

The man who had spoken was Carl Miller, the captain of the prison guards. He was in his early thirties, and his dark uniform was trimly tailored to his powerful physique. His eyes were narrow slits over his high cheekbones, and his thin lips were hard and cruel.

"Sorry to be leaving us, Rocky?"

"Yeah," Rocky sneered.

"Yes, sir!" one of the guards barked, and struck the youth

viciously in the pit of the stomach.

Rocky doubled over under the force of the blow, then caught his breath and straightened slowly. "Yes, sir," he said.

"That's better," Miller smiled thinly, lighting a cigarette. "I bet your buddies around here are going to miss you."

"I dunno, sir—maybe."

"Sure they will, Rocky. Especially when they get hot for being screwed. I hear you're quite a lover, kid. Right?"

"I dunno, sir."

"The hell you don't know!" Miller smashed his cigarette into an ash tray and stepped back. "Okay, boys, loosen him up a little."

Instantly the two guards fell on the youth, pounding him with their fists. He tried to defend himself but it was useless, and they struck him again and again. One of them brought the heel of his boot down on Rocky's bare toes brutally, and the youth choked back a cry of pain. Then he felt a hand strike hard against the inside of his thigh, just missing his genitals.

"That's enough. Let him sit down."

Rocky sagged into the chair they thrust behind him and sat there, doubled over and gasping for breath. Suddenly Miller grabbed him by the hair and jerked his head back.

"Feel more like talking, Rocky?"

"Yes, sir," the youth muttered numbly.

"Good," Miller smiled, releasing his hair. "Now let's hear about what you've been doing for kicks. You've been pretty friendly with the new kid Billy Fisher, haven't you?"

"Yes, sir."

"Let's see—you're nineteen and he's only sixteen. I bet he's damn nice! Hell, I bet you were his first, right?"

"Yes, sir."

"Tell us what happened, Rocky."

"I just got in bed with him one night. That's all, sir."

Miller chuckled. "That's why we make you guys turn in your clothes every night, Rocky. It makes it harder for you to escape and easier to get your rocks off! Well, what happened when he got it hard?"

"I took care of it, sir," Rocky muttered.

"You mean you sucked his cock? Say it."

"I sucked his cock."

"And he sucked yours?"

"Yes, sir."

"You really are a lover!" Miller snickered. "You milked down his virgin load and then you got him to drink your cream! Shit, I bet you rolled him over and jammed your hammer between his cheeks too, didn't you!"

Rocky shook his head vigorously. "No sir, I didn't screw him. He's just a kid!"

Miller chuckled as one of the guards began to laugh. "A sixteen-year old virgin piece of ass and you didn't fuck him? Damnit, you're dumb! I think we better wise you up a little!" He moved around behind the seated youth and began rubbing his hands over Rocky's solid shoulders. "You didn't stay with us very long this time, and you kept your nose clean so we didn't have a chance to teach you very much. That's why I thought we'd have a little party down here tonight—sort of a farewell party." He moved his hands over the youth's shirt and then began to unbutton the buttons. "We'll give you your own clothes back after the party, so you won't need this uniform any more." He spread the shirt open and thrust his hands inside, running them slowly over the warm, firm flesh. "You're a well-built young stud, Rocky. I bet you really know how to show a guy a good time! Well, we're going to show you a few things too!" He stepped back with a short laugh. "Okay, boys, take off his shirt and hang him up!"

Miller turned and sauntered from the room as the two guards came forward and dragged Rocky to his feet.

"Off with the shirt, kid," one of them grinned. "No use getting it covered with blood."

This is it, Rocky thought, as he shrugged off his shirt. He had seen the guards beat other prisoners until they screamed for mercy. He grit his teeth; he wouldn't give them that satisfaction!

The youth had sleek, strongly muscled shoulders and arms, and his neatly curved chest was sparsely covered with soft, dark hair. His smooth flesh was a golden-tan in color, and his physique was a handsome blend of youthful virility and rugged maturity.

"Damn nice!" the guard smiled approvingly, placing one hand on Rocky's chest and rubbing it over the warm flesh slowly. "I bet you could be real nice if you wanted to. We could all go up to Carl's room and have a few drinks, and then you could show us what a fine young lover you are." He moistened his lips eagerly. "That'd be better than getting the piss beat out of you, wouldn't it?"

Rocky stared at the man coldly. "Drop your pants and bend over, and I'll show you what kind of a lover I am!"

Still grinning, the guard shrugged. "Have it your own way, kid. You think you're pretty tough, but it won't take long to make you crawl. When we get done, even your hard-up buddies in the showers wouldn't fuck you on a bet!"

The guards forced Rocky to stand with his legs spread wide while they chained his ankles to two studs set several feet apart in the floor. Then they lowered ropes from the ceiling and attached them to the handcuffs they snapped around his wrists. Tightening the ropes again, they jerked Rocky's arms over his head, pulling his body up taut and helpless.

"Shit, that's a fine target," one of the guards chuckled, wiping his palms across Rocky's solid, muscle-ridged back. Then he stepped up close and ripped the youth's trim butt. "That's just the right height, too!"

Suddenly the door opened and Carl Miller came in again. His face was flushed and glistened with perspiration, and he carried a bottle of whiskey in one hand. He surveyed Rocky with a thin grin and tugged at the bulging crotch of his trousers.

"All ready for our party, Rocky?" He handed the bottle to one of the guards and stood directly in front of the youth. "I just had a little drink with your buddy Billy. He isn't much of a drinker yet, but he'll learn." Gazing directly into Rocky's eyes, Miller began to unbutton his shirt as he continued. "He's a pretty hot little kid. He's sure going to miss those nights in the rack with you!" He peeled off his shirt and flexed his arms slowly. He was powerfully muscled, and his solid, barreled chest was matted with black hair that grew down over his belly to the low-hanging waist of his trousers. "You don't look very happy, Rocky. Boys, let's warm him up!"

Miller stepped back, folding his arms across his chest and grinning as the two guards came forward. They had both stripped to the waist and were strongly developed, and each held a short length of rubber hose. One of them tapped his piece of hose lightly against the helpless youth's crotch and snickered.

"That'll cool you off for a while, huh, stud?"

Then he drew back, took careful aim, and struck him hard in the pit of the stomach. Rocky clenched his teeth, and then a violent blow smashed him from behind over the kidneys. Again and again they hammered him, and his body was shaken by the force and pain of each blow. Someone hit him across the face, and there was the warm, salty taste of blood in his mouth. His brain began to reel, and then from a long way off, he heard Miller call a halt to the beating.

They let him hang there resting for a few minutes, and the sharp pains slowly dulled into an aching numbness. At last he opened his eyes and saw the three men grinning at him. The two guards were breathing hard, and a light sweat glistened over their naked torsos.

"You don't look so good, Rocky," Miller snickered, stepping forward. He held a damp towel, and carefully wiped it over the youth's face. It came away stained with crimson. "Maybe you don't feel so good either," he went on, rubbing the towel over Rocky's chest and wide armpits.

"Maybe we're too rough for him," one of the guards chuckled, slapping the hose against his open palm.

"Are we too rough, Rocky?"

Rocky moistened his lips slowly. "No, sir."

"That's right," Miller smiled, "Rocky's plenty tough. You're not afraid of anything are you, kid?" He dropped one hand to the youth's crotch and began rubbing his fingers over his fly. "Like that, Rocky? Feels pretty good huh? Well, let's see what you've got!" Slowly he unfastened Rocky's trousers and pushed them down to his ankles. "There!"

Like all the prisoners, Rocky wore no shorts, and now he was completely naked. The muscles of his thighs and legs stood up solid beneath his smoothly tanned flesh, and his strong, mature genitals hung loose and full from the nest of tangled black hair at his groin.

"Hey, he's really loaded!" one of the guards exclaimed.

"Yeah," Miller nodded. "I haven't had a chance to play with a young beauty like you in a long time, Rocky." He wiped the towel over the youth's thick, relaxed cock and large, firm balls carefully. "That's a damn fine piece of meat. No wonder Billy didn't mind going down on it!" He dropped the towel and brought his hands up along Rocky's thighs, gripping his smooth, heavy dick in one hand and his slippery nuts in the other. "I bet those eggs churn up one hell of a milkshake! How'd you like to have a pair of hot lips taking a drink right about now?"

Rocky glared at the man. "Go ahead and try it—I'll give you a throatful of piss!"

"That's no way to talk," Miller said calmly, twisting Rocky's balls sharply and grinning as the youth winced. "I fixed up this little party so you could have a good time. I even brought Billy down here so he could say good-bye to you." He nodded to the guards. "Get the kid—he's down the hall."

The guards returned after a moment, bringing a slim, shirtless youth into the room with them. His body was youthfully trim and neat, and he swayed drunkenly as he stared at Rocky with glazed eyes.

"Hi Rocky," he grinned.

"Hi, Billy."

"Rocky's been telling us about you two guys," Miller said, with a cold smile. "He says you really know the score, Billy." He turned to the two guards. "Take his pants down."

"Cut it out, Miller!" Rocky exclaimed. "Leave the kid alone!"

Miller snickered, and Rocky watched helplessly while the men stripped the drunken boy. A moment later Billy was naked, youthfully innocent of the eyes surveying his sleek, attractive body hungrily. Then Miller grabbed him and pushed him up flat against Rocky.

"That's the way you guys like to be, isn't it? Belly to belly, right?" Miller gripped Billy by the shoulders. "Let's see what Rocky taught you!" He pushed the boy down on his knees in front of Rocky. "Now, kiss his dick! Make love to it!"

Billy stared at the heavy, relaxed organs hanging from his friend's groin and then bent forward, letting his lips rub lightly over the smooth head of Rocky's cock.

"And his balls!"

Billy lifted Rocky's powerful dick and kissed each ball tenderly.

"Now suck on him! Make that hot tool show what it can do!"

Obediently, Billy held the organ up and ran his tongue over the flange slowly. Then he opened his lips and eased it into his mouth.

Miller stepped back wiping his hands over his powerful, hair-matted chest and then he began unfastening his trousers slowly. Grinning steadily, he pushed his pants down and pulled at the massive bulge in the crotch of his shorts. Then he dropped his shorts and kicked his clothes from around his ankles. His legs were thick and hard, and his cock hung down long and loose over his large balls. He grasped his dick and began stroking it proudly.

"Here's something no kid can give you, Rocky!" Slowly the heavy organ stiffened until it stood erect, a huge column of throbbing flesh topped by a bullet-shaped head that seemed to gleam with hardness. "I get plenty hot working on a guy like you, and you're going to cool it off every time!"

His eyes flashing with expectation, Miller walked slowly around behind Rocky, rubbing his hands over the youth's sleek, muscle-ridged back. "If I didn't have to turn you loose afterward, I'd see how you like the feel of my belt across your back. But we don't want to mark you up, do we?" He wrapped his arms about Rocky's waist and thrust his huge, solid cock between the youth's thighs. "Still hot, kid?" he asked, as he slid his hands down over Rocky's flat belly to his groin. "Shit, you sure stay hard a long time!" he murmured, gripping the youth's rigid dick with one hand and his loose-hanging balls with the other. "Still thinking about how Billy sucked your prick? Well, relax and I'll fix you up."

Rocky stood there, his wrists fastened to the ropes over his head, his ankles chained to the floor, and he closed his eyes and grit his teeth as Miller began stroking his tense rod. He felt the man's warm, solid body pressing against his back, the muscular arms wrapped tightly about him, the fingers playing with his nuts and massaging his dick steadily, the giant probe rubbing between his legs, the crisp pubic hairs against his butt. Miller's hand moved up and down the youth's throbbing pole faster and faster, until Rocky could feel the first watery juices begin to drip from it.

"C'mon, kid!" Miller barked, "I'm gonna make you squirt everything you've got!"

Rocky's body tensed, and he threw his head back and gasped with the excitement of his approaching climax. Miller knew that the pressure inside the youth had reached the boiling point, and he chuckled as he felt his prisoner's cock quiver tensely. Then he dug his fingers into Rocky's heavy nuts and twisted them brutally.

Rocky's hoarse groans of pleasure suddenly became an agonized cry as the crippling pain tore up through him from his crotch, and then the hot, sticky cream was spurting from his dick wildly. The tortured youth tore helplessly at the chains holding his wrists and ankles as the thick juice spattered from inside him and the fingers continued to squeeze his balls ruthlessly.

"Shit, you must have drowned that kid!" Miller murmured as the potent organ gave a final powerful jerk and the tremendous flow of rich cream came to a halt. He gave Rocky's nuts a last vicious twist and then released him. "Still feel tough, kid?"

Rocky's chin dropped to his chest, and he moaned softly as the fierce pain gave way to a racking numbness. He felt the man behind him slowly step back. Then strong fingers were spreading the cheeks of his ass, and a huge, solid pole was pressing between them. He felt the massive, dripping head thrust roughly against the hps of his hole, and he jerked up on his toes to escape it.

"Relax, kid, you're no virgin!" Miller muttered hoarsely. "I'm going to shove it to you bare! I'm going to fuck you nice and slow until you think you're going crazy, and when I come, it'll feel like a bomb exploding inside you! And then I'm going to beat you where it hurts the most! I'm going to cripple you good, Rocky, and every time I get hard, I'm going to jam it into you!" He gripped the youth by the hips and pressed them down as he brought the iron-hard knob smashing up against the taut asshole. "Get ready to scream, kid! Here it comes!"

* * * * * * *

Rocky stood naked in the bathroom, staring at his reflection in the full-length minor. Carefully he examined the freshly healed scar on his face, and then he stepped back and smiled proudly at the handsome, athletic figure in the glass. He spread his legs wide and stretched hard, and then he chuckled as he jerked his hips forward and back, watching his thick, relaxed cock swing heavily between his thighs. Suddenly the doorbell rang sharply, and he pulled on a bathrobe as he hurried to answer it.

"Hello, Rocky." It was Carl Miller.

"What the hell do you want?"

Miller tried an uncertain grin. "Lemme come in. I just want to see how you're doing."

Rocky shrugged and stepped back. "Okay, c'mon in."

Miller closed the door behind him and handed the youth a bottle. "I thought we could have a drink."

Rocky looked at the officer thoughtfully for a moment, then shrugged again. "Okay, make yourself at home. I'll get a couple of glasses."

Miller took off his coat and tie and followed the youth into the kitchen.

"You sure look good, kid."

"I heal fast," Rocky muttered, pouring the drinks, living room for some time. Finally Rocky got to his feet. Miller refilled their drinks, he made them quite strong. Then they talked in the living room for some time. Finally Rocky got to his feet.

"Look, Carl, I've got to get dressed."

"Got a date?"

"Maybe." Rocky sauntered into the bedroom. "Why?"

Miller stood up and followed him. "I figured we could have some more drinks, or maybe go up to my place."

"So you can beat me up again, maybe?"

Miller stood behind Rocky and put his hands on the youth's shoulders, "I want to make love to you, Rocky!" he blurted out. "I want to spend the night in bed with you!" Suddenly his arms were around Rocky and his strong fingers were ripping open his robe and running over his smooth, solid torso. "I want you, kid—all the way!" His hand slid down to the youth's crotch and caressed his powerful organs, and then he grasped the handsome cock firmly. "I want you to fuck me, Rocky!"

Rocky stood in silence for a moment and then sucked in a deep breath. "Okay, Carl. Take off your clothes."

Rocky went into the kitchen and filled their glasses once more. When he returned, Carl lay naked and tense with anticipation on the bed.

"No Vaseline, no nothing, Carl."

"Anything you say, Rocky."

Rocky stripped off his robe, and as he threw it aside, he noticed Miller's trousers tossed over the back of a chair. Slowly he picked them up and pulled the belt loose from them. Then he stared at Miller.

"Roll over on your belly, Carl."

Miller gazed up at the naked youth for a moment. Rocky's handsome features were set and determined, and his dark eyes flashed with excitement. His strong young body was tense, and Miller could see the powerful cock begin to stiffen with throbbing strength. Then Miller was staring at the youth's solidly muscled arm and the fingers tightly gripping the black leather belt. Slowly he moistened his lips and nodded.

"Anything you say, Rocky," he repeated softly.

ABOUT THE AUTHOR

V. J. BANIS is the critically acclaimed author ("the master's touch in storytelling..."—*Publishers Weekly*) of more than 200 published books and numerous short stories in a career spanning nearly a half century. A native of Ohio and a longtime Californian, he lives and writes now in West Virginia's beautiful Blue Ridge.

You can visit him at http://www.vjbanis.com